THE BOUNCING HILLS

THE BOUNCING HILLS

BY THE SAME AUTHOR

illustrated by Edmund Julian

The BOUNCING HILLS

Dialect Tales and Light Verse
by Jack Clemo

"I hear the bouncing hills
Grow larked......"

- DYLAN THOMAS

ISBN Hardback 0 907566 39 1
ISBN Paperback 0 907566 38 3

Printed by: Helston Printers, 12 Wendron Street, Helston, Cornwall.

Published by: Dyllansow Truran, Cornish Publications, Redruth, Cornwall.

CONTENTS

PREFACE

DIALECT STORIES:

HUMOROUS VERSE:

PREFACE

With the exception of "Noah's Tortoise" all these tales were first published during the 1930's in Cornish almanacks - *Saundry's Almanack* at Penzance, *Netherton's Almanack* at Truro, or *One and All Almanack* at Camborne. They are reissued not only because they show a side of my talent which has been neglected in later years, but also because they preserve the homely and cheerful aura of village life in the china clay country as it was fifty years ago.

The humorous verse is more recent and has not been published before. Some of it was written to amuse children, and this involved an occasional widening of range to include Dorset as well as Cornwall, since I have had child-friends in Weymouth. The rhymes about television filming were touched off by the making of the B.B.C. drama-documentary film of my early life, "A Different Drummer," in September 1979. The two poems, "Lane Traffic" and "Slag Vision" - not strictly comic but capturing happy memories of my childhood -appeared in the *Cornish Banner*.

J.C.

8

MARIA AND THE MILKMAN

Sammy Chegwidden had traapsed around Pengooth village four times that evening afore he catched sight o' Maria Blake; and he wad'n much better off when he did see her.

'Twas out beginning the lane that they mit, where the village ended, and nobody could'n see 'em. Maria'd bin pickin' smutties and was carrying a gurt pile in her arms, wearing a ole sack over her dress to catch the dirt.

Sammy listened to her taale without saying a word, but soon's she finished he shawed that he wad'n pleased 'bout it.

"You'm a purty maid, you be," says he, scoffing. "Makin' outs you love me an' yet willin' fer another chap......"

"I bean't willin', as I've told 'ee," says Maria, glaazen hard to a telegraph pole on the hedge. "But wot can I do? I've told Ginger Neale times and times that I woan't 'ave un, but he doan't take no notice. He's allis pesterin' me and I caan't git rids of un."

"I doan't bleeve you want to, in the bottom," says Sammy, all s'picious. "If you maade it plain to un......"

"I 'ave," says Maria, beginning to pant. "So plain as daylight, Sammy. But he woan't see it. Whenever I go out he's waitin' around - everybody in the village knaw it an' think I'm goin' 'ave un."

"Well, if you come walking with me he woan't be able to butt in, will a?"

"No, but - people'd say I was flirtin', knawing like they do how Ginger belong hangin' round me."

"Never mind wot people said!" snaps Sammy. "If you do love me......"

"Well, if ever you see me go past your plaace be meself, you can come out. That's outside the village, and we need'n go far. Ther' might be a chance, but nobody mus'n knaw till......" A thought come to her and she hugged up her bundle o' smutties like if 'twas a baaby. "Look, Sammy, if you can find some way to maake Ginger stop pesterin' me, I'll go weth 'ee, sure 'nuff. While he's on like this I'm tied hand an' foot.

There's me poor mawther to think of - she suffer bad weth her heart and could'n stick the shock of it if it got out that I was flirtin'."

Sammy glaazed up to the sky for a minute - coming rain 'twas, clouds lowering; the wind gitting up, too, nipping cold. Then he says, purty excited:

"I knaw, Maria! Neale' the milkman, edd'n a?"

"Course he is, but that aan't got nort......"

"You jist wait a day or two," says Sammy, all mysterious. "You'll be minse yet, Maria darlint, an' afore many weeks is past there'll be wedding bells ringin' in the future!"

Sammy went off home some proud, and all that evening he was thinking out his plan. If he could knack Neale's custom the fella'd go smash, and then he would'n have nort to offer Maria and would leave her quiet. But how could he knack Neale without risking his own neck? Make people believe Neale was charging of 'em too much for the traade they bought of un; or better still, make 'em think his stuff wad'n no cop at all - suggest as how he watered his milk, for instance! Once the idea come to un to try and take away Neale's custom by going in for the farm business hisself, seeing as he were out o' work; but he soon seed that that was out o' the question. No, he must go around quiet, drop a hint here and there, casual-like, so as not to rouse no s'picions - and see what happened.

The folleyin' day he put his resolve in action, making a start in his own house. Tay-time 'twas, when he was setting fore to table with his mother and young brother, Freddie. Same as usual, the woman had cut a slice o' bread'n-butter and put it 'pon his plate. Sammy glaazed at it a minute, then took it up between his thumb and li'l finger. He bite off a bit, then put the slice back on his plate and made a face.

Mrs. Chegwidden seed to once that something was wrong. "Wot's matter?" ax she, leaning fore across the table.

"The butter," groans Sammy, wrinkling up his nose. "Awful strong or some'ing, edd'n it? Ted'n taastin' right somehow."

"Git along!" says the woman, picking up the traade and smiling to it. "Ther' edd'n nort wrong weth the butter. Tes yer stomach sour, Sammy, or yer temper. Wot'll ee 'ave nex?"

"Piece o' crame an' sugar," answers Sammy, and he said it in sich a funny sort o' voice that both his mother and brother glaazed hard at un for over a minute. Then without saying a word the woman spread his cream and flinked sugar over it.

Soon's 'twas put on his plate Sammy took it up, turning it over and over, and sniffing. At last he ventured to dig his teeth in one li'l corner o' the crest - and next minute he'd scat the chair flying and was tearing fore to the stove and leaning in over the ash-box like if he was goin' be sick.

"Wotever - !" gasp the woman. She was fitty scared, and Freddie'd half rised from his chair and made ready to scoot, 'fraid that Sammy was goin' git ramping.

"That crame! That crame!" spluttered Sammy, his head going from side to side. "Tes gone poor I tell ee! Ugh!" And he made outs to urge.

Mrs. Chegwidden was gitting a bit vexed by now. "You'm making a fool o' yerself over nothin'," snaps she. "That there crame is so sweet as I be - I 'ad a piece meself not ten minutes ago. You'm on 'pon some mischief, Sammy."

"No sich thing!" screech Sammy, rocking to and fro over the ash-box and holding his head. "I've tho't fer weeks there bin some'ing wrong weth the deery traade we been having. I aan't said nort, I sticked it so long as I could, but now tes got that I caan't hold in no longer."

The woman turned to Freddie. "You aan't taste nort wrong with it, 'ave ee? You'd be sure to spake if twad'n tasting fitty."

Freddie was glazing to his brother, a bit frightened. He feeled twad'n safe to deny what Sammy was saying, though o' course he had'n found nort wrong with the stuff. "I - I dunnaw 'bout the crame," says he, some flustered, "but I bleeve I ded think the beef in me pasty yes'day was gone bit pindy."

Sammy swinged around and clout un 'cross the nuddik. "You thickhead!" he shouted. "We bean't talkin' 'bout the *butcher*; tes Neale the milkman, and mawther got to finish wid'n to-morra."

"I bean't goin' to, then!" snaps his mother, firing up. "The fault's weth yer appetite, me sen."

"Es it?" says Sammy, vicious, and he haaled the chair for to table again and squabbed down. "Hand here a slab o' saffern caake an' you'll see whe'er I got a appetite or no." And bless ee if he did'n git rids o' that chunk o' cake in less'n a minute!"

'Twas fair mystifying and the woman could'n make it up. Sammy was grizzling away to hisself all secret: she knawed he had some plan or other working away at, but could'n tell what twas.

"Be that as may," she says when he'd finished the cake, "you doan't catch me changin' milkmen jist to plaze one o' yer fads. You'm so pernickety 'bout what you do ate......"

"You lost yer taasters, that's wot tes," ansers Sammy, glowing at her. "You'd ate half-a-pound o' vinnid cheese an' not knaw ther' was ort wrong with et."

"Wot 'bout Freddie?"

"He's 'fraid to awn up, cause he knaw you'd give un a lacing, but I've maade up me awn mind......"

"Tes aunly the crame and butter, anyhow," says Mrs. Chegwidden. "The milk......"

But fore she could finish there come a splutter and Sammy's tay-cup shoot 'cross the table. He'd took a zoop at the tay and there twas dribbling all over his chin - he could'n clunk it down.

"Sammy!" his mother burst out, desperate.

"Mawther!" gasp Sammy, wriggling in his chair and try-to hold his mouth abroad. "You got to finish weth Ginger Neale - 'morra morning. This milk - I never taaste nort like it. However you can clunk that......"

"You'm dotty," says his mother, withering; she glazed down in his tay-cup what he'd shuv'd up agin her elbaw. Freddie got up and renned from the room, 'fraid what was goin' happen next. "Must be yer clunkers - unless you'm putting it all on. You bean't thusty I doan't bleeve."

"Empt' out the milk from that tay an' I'll toss it off in one clunk," Sammy ansers, feverish. "The milk is curdled, gone so sour as......"

He was looking to the tay proper taisy. His mother happened to glance out the winda. She glimpsed somebody's yella hat over the garden wall, and rised up quick to see who was passing. She wanted to turn the talk off to other matters - she'd had 'nuff o' Sammy's antics.

"Maid jist gone by outside," says she. "Maria Blake I bleeve."

"Hey?" Sammy scared her wuss'n ever by what he done next. He jumped up and reshed across to the door and down to gate like a mazed man. Mrs. Chegwidden seed un sticked up outside, his hair flying in the wind, glaazen fust one way and then t'other.

Arter a spur he come back in some flurrik. "Tes no sich thing - she edd'n out there," he holla'd out. "Wot ded ee want to 'ave me on like that for?"

"Aw" says the woman, all quiet, glaazen at the bread'n-butter, the crame-and-sugar and the tay: she seed a bit o' daylight in 'em now. "So that's of it, is it? Tho't you bin all quiet lately. Tes a maid - Maria Blake."

Sammy coloured up, looking ratty. He ded'n said nothing, but he come fore to the chair and was making to sit down again, trembling like a jelly. But his mother says:

"I never maade it up 'toal. She *is* jist gone along outside - up around the corner spoase, aunly you'm so silly you ded'n think o' looking that way."

The seat o' Sammy's trousers had titched the cushion, but 'pon that he bobbed up again like lightning and way-to-go. He jaaced fore past the garden wall to the corner and dashed around un, kipping in close agin the hedge to save time. But as it happened it hold un up instead. He stepped on something and next thing he knawed two raws o' teeth was hanging on to his leg. Sammy yowled out, glaazen down to see what twas. A dog - black-and-white terrier. Sammy screeched and danced around in the road but twas several minutes for the cretture left go. Then he glanced up the road - and his eyes fair start out o' their sockets. Up li'l way, standing still and glaazen back at'n, was Maria and Ginger Neale!

Sammy seed red for a minute. His leg was hurting of'n a bit, but he stanked up the road, hobbling on at some rate. 'Fore he got to 'em he started letting off steam.

"That's your dog, edd'n et?"

"Tes my dog," ansers Ginger, frowning.

"Well, I'm goin' report un to the p'lice," says Sammy. "E's dangerous. See 'ow 'e grabbed hold o' me leg." Twad'n till then that he dared to look at the maid - and he had a fright. She was looking vexed 'nuff to scat un down; and when she spoke 'twas a proper snap.

"Sarve ee right!" she said to un. "Taaren round the corner like that. You was like a maaze man - no wonder he bite ee; I'd 'ave done the saame if I'd bin he."

Something must be up! S'poase she was vexed cause he'd catched her with Ginger. But if twas that, she must have told un a pack o' lies. And Sammy says, all stiff:

"Aw. Who do ee think you'm talkin' to?"

"That's right," says the maid, mocking. "Maake outs you doan't knaw me - say you ded'n want me to go courtin'...... Here! wot be ee doing of?"

Sammy, feeling waik all of a sudden, had cluckied down in the road and rolled up his trousers leg: he was beginning to pull down his socks. Maria glaazed for a croom, then flared up indignant.

"You'm acting insultin', shawing yer legs there in middle the road fer everybody to see. I'll report you to the p'lice if you doan't git up and go in to once."

Sammy got down on one knee and waved his fist up at her. "Tes the dog," says he. "I bleeve me leg's bliddin'." His voice was all choky, partly with rage and partly - well, Sammy was a bit upset, as you might expect.

"I hope ee is," the maid rapped out. "Twill teach ee a lesson. I knaw wot you was on upon. You'd seed me go along and was coming arter me, you imperent old toad!"

Ginger was glaazen at her all the time she was speaking, proper flabbergasted. He'd never heard Maria carr' on like this afore, and he feeled uncomfor'ble, I can tell ee. At last he says, all 'oarse:

"No need to git rampin' about it, Maria."

"Aw, edd'n ther'?" says the maid, whizzing around 'pon un. "That's all you knaw about it. If you knawed as I do 'ow he've pestered me......"

"So you doan't want neither one of us?" says Ginger, sharp-like.

"Never mind wot I do want fer the minute; 'tis best to settle this business so far's he's concerned." She stamped her feet, coming close up agin Sammy, and he shrinked back, 'fraid she was goin' kick un. He was glaazen hard to his ankle - li'l red mark there, but no blood. His hands was fumbling around the bottom of his pants. They seed that he was sweating streams, and no wonder. He'd never have believed it! Whatever could have took the maid he ded'n knaw. And she went on raging as if she was never goin' stop.

"So well for ee to knaw wot I'd be like to ee, then praps you woan't be so maaze to 'ave me. Aw yes, ole fella, you seemed to think I was a li'l worm to tread 'pon, but even a worm'll twinkle if you step 'pon un."

"You bean't twinklin'," says Sammy, all gruff; "you'm blaazin'." He shuv'd his mouth fore quick bunk agin his knee, but that did'n stop the words coming out.

"Ess, I'm a blaazer all right, when I got to deal with sich idjits as you. Git up, do ee hear, or I'll slap yer chacks for ee!"

Slawly Sammy pulled up his sock and rised to his feet, shaking. He looked hard to Ginger for a tick or two, then to the dog what was eyeing of un all s'picious from in behind a fuzzy-bush. Ginger says, bottling up his feelings:

"You better go in I reckon. You've worked her up."

"Twas your old dog what done it!" Sammy burst out, and he stooped quick, grabbed a stone in the road and drawed at the crettur. "An' I'm goin' report......"

"You best not to!" shouts the maid, red in the face. "You report Ginger's dog and I'll never spake to ee again so long as I live."

Sammy tried to make a face at her, but couldn' manage it, so he turned around. "You need'n," says he, very low. "I've found out wot you be, anyhow. I knaw wot fibs you've a-told me. You want Ginger, not me. Oall right; he's the wuss off. Good riddance to ee!" And he stanked away back the road, forgetting that his leg was bite.

He was in a proper mizz-maze all evening: did'n knaw what to do next. What was the good o' smashing Neale if Maria did'n want un? No cop 'tall - but Sammy mained to do it, if only to have his spite out on the both of 'em. Twas plain as a pike-staff that the maid had been making game of un all along; yet she'd seemed sincere 'nuff in it. Sammy was proper dithered and could'n make head nor tail o' the business.

Next morning he made sure to be in when Neale come with the milk. When Ginger knacked to door Sammy stride back, grim as granite.

"Here, I got some'ing to tell you," says he, very curt. "Our people's finishin'......"

Ginger interrupted, talking 'bout something else. "Well, Sammy," he says, "you got yer chance."

"Wot do ee main?" ax Sammy, snapping his eyes.

"That there maid Blake......"

Sammy waved the empty jug over his head. "Doan't you mention her name to me," he says. "I've had 'nuff o' she to last me a lifetime."

"You doan't want her then?" ax Ginger, and he burst out laffing.

"That's a clane swipe for her that is! She woan't have nobody now."

"Wot - you've finished weth her?"

"Course I 'ave, arter seein' wot a gashly old temper she got. It opened me eyes. I bean't goin' let meself in fer that, not if I knaw it!"

Sammy glaazed down in the jug as Ginger tipped out the milk in un. His hand was shaking and when the jug got nearly full he beginned floxin' it out 'pon the doorstep.

"She've got paid out now, anyway," says he, all savage. "Spoase she screeched when you towld her and said she would never act like that to you; eh?"

"No, there wad'n very much fuss weth her; she took it sulky and said if I would'n 'ave no more to do weth her I could plaze meself - it did'n maake no difference to she! A touchy sort o' maid - I pity the bloke who *do* have her! Twon't bc mc ner you, anyhow."

"No fear!" says Sammy, but he spoke all quavery, like if he was sorry 'bout something - and all of a sudden a tear come to his left eye and trookled down over his chack. 'Fore he could wipe un away ee'd splashed down in the milk.

Ginger turned and leaved un glaazen like a stewed owl in the jug.

That very evening, as Sammy was trudging home from the village, he seed Maria traapsing droo the fields jist ahead, making for a stile round the corner in front of un. He glowed for a croom, standing still in the roadway, in two minds whe'er to go on and face her or scoot back some other way. But if did'n take un long to decide. "I woan't be bait!" says he to hisself. "I'll go straight on and woan't look at her." And on he went with his head cocked up, pouching out his mouth and trying to look at'n.

Maria come out to the stile, and be time he got to the corner she was sticked up in the ditch, no hat on, smiling, Sammy did'n look - kipt his eyes turned down and stride along with arms flying. Next thing he knawed he'd bunked into something - not a dog this time, but a maid! Maria'd stepped for right in front of un.

"Wot be ee runnin' away for?" ax she, all husky.

Sammy glowed, red as a beet. "An' wot be you comin' arter me for, I should like to knaw. I've had 'bout 'nuff o' you. Walking out with Ginger like you did......"

The maid squeezed his arm. " I could'n help it, Sammy, sure 'nuff," says she, some anxious. "I'd bin to A'nt Jaanie's all arternoon and was on me way back to the village when Ginger catched up weth me jist as I got in sight o' your housen I could'n turn and go back and 'ad to go 'long weth un, cause he would'n leave me to meself. I 'oped as 'ow you would'n see me and was feeling some vexed over it."

"Seems so, be the way you carr'd on," Sammy says, all short. He was panting and could'n take his eyes off her face.

She laffed. "Aw, you old silly, how ded'n ee see droo it?"

"See droo wot?" gasp Sammy, glaazen straight at her noase with one eye shut.

"Why, me acting like that. I feeled sure you'd be tickled. It come to me soon's I seed ee come around the corner. I tho't if I made outs to be some gashly Ginger'd 'ave a eye-opener and would'n want no more to do with me. An' it worked, did'n it?"

"You main - that was your way o' gittin rids of un? You done it all because you - you'm willin' to go with me?"

"That depend 'pon you, whe'er we'm goin' together or no," says Maria, pulling his arm round her waist. "One thing I can 'sure ee, Sammy - last night you 'ad all the jawin' you'll ever git from me - and I ded'n main it, even then!"

MRS. STROUT'S MATCH-MAKING

Tom Gumma screened hisself by the shrubs overhanging a corner outside the last house o' Pengooth churchtown, and listened. Twad'n the first time he'd hide around thikky place, but he'd never waited there feeling so wisht as he did now. 'Twas early afternoon of a December day, very cold and gloomy, and Tom did'n expect to hear nothing what would bring sunshine to un.

He heard Mrs. 'Arris talking to her neighbour, Mrs. Strout.

Mrs. 'Arris was stanning agin the ole stone wall what divided her path from Mrs. Strout's, and Mrs. Strout was lopping in her doorway. Mrs. 'Arris had been glaazen around the sky, and at last she pointed upward.

"Do look as if tis coming snaw, Mrs. Strout," says she. "I 'ope you woan't git catched in it comin' back from town."

"I was maning to taake a short cut," says Mrs. Strout, rubbing the murfles on her chacks. "Tis a long ole jank around the road from Trebilcock's corner, where bus do stop. I tho't I'd cut in across claywork tanks - saave a quarter mile."

Mrs. 'Arris wagged her bare head warning. "They ole steps be some skittery now frost is come," she says. "And you'll be loaded up wi' parcels, I daresay."

"Iss, braave bit to be bo't," ansers Mrs. Strout. "Chrismus is near, an' several neighbours 'ave give orders to me o' zummin they do want."

"Lobbs, I s'poase?" ax Mrs. 'Arris, drawing herself up like a poker.

"More'n they," says Mrs. Strout.

"Well, as I was sayin', tis risky comin' back along thews tanks - like a glass bottle wi' the frost, an' a broke leg bean't no nice Chrismus present."

"No, nor tedd'n," agreed Mrs. Strout. "I should'n a-risked it, if

Maaster Lobb ded'n belong working there."

Mrs. 'Arris stooped down and bobbed up again quick. "Aw. Wot will 'e do? You'm too fat, Mrs. Strout......"

"'E edd'n goin' carr' me," says Mrs. Strout, looking some vexed to her neighbour, and laying hold to a broom resting agin the door durn. "Only 'elp me up ovver they steps. 'E's arternoon core there this week, and we talked about it over there last night."

"Where - over round the tanks?"

Mrs. Strout glaazed to Mrs. 'Arris withering, and flurrik'd the broom at her. "Doan't ee knaw we do go visiting they Lobbs?" she axed.

"Tis gittin' a bit thick, I've 'eard," ansers Mrs. 'Arris, sniffing. "You d'go along braave an' offen of a evenin', doan't ee - Ivy too?"

"Iss. and she do dearly like it ovver to Lobbs', the maid do. There's a baaby there, y'knaw, an' a wireless, besides the children."

Mrs. 'Arris clunked hard and squitched around, looking a bit niffid. "I should'n 'ave incouraged that if I'd bin you," she says, all s'picious.

"Incouraged wot?" says Mrs. Strout, indignant.

Mrs. 'Arris stanked up towards her, waving a arm. "If Ivy be gittin' to like goin' there," she says deliberate, "tis most likely 'cause Wilf be gittin' to like she."

Mrs. Strout scratched her pluffy face, pooching out her lips. "I've never seed no sign, Mrs. 'Arris - not even a joke between 'e an' Ivy 'pon sich a matter."

"Well, that's a bad sign," says Mrs. 'Arris. "When there bean't no jokes you may depend ther's zummin they doan't want other foaks to knaw. Tis a guilty sign, Mrs. Strout, an' I'm susprised that you abben done nort about it."

"Ivy bean't no chiel now - she's seb'mteen, an' can go where she plaze," retorted Mrs. Strout.

Mrs. 'Arris shaked her fist over the wall. "If you had'n started goin' to Lobbs she'd never a-got inside the'r 'ouse at 'oall," cried Mrs. 'Arris.

Mrs. Strout eyed her warily. "Ivy'd a-mit Wilf outside, any'ow, an' if Tom Gumma caan't look arter his awn courtin'......"

"You'm slocking Ivy away from un, that's wot you'm doin'," declared Mrs. 'Arris, her breath coming quick and her face going purple. "There wi' the wireless an' the baaby an' Wilf so offen - no wonder she edd'n so maazed about Tommy."

"She never was maazed about un," says Mrs. Strout, very quiet. "An' I never took no fancy to un meself. Twould be 'ard 'pon Ivy if I ded'n try to do zummin now he've lost 'is job."

"Wilf'll lost 'is job next," says Mrs. 'Arris, prophetic. "I 'ope 'e do, an' then poor ole Tommy......"

Mrs. Strout turned back indoors. "Never mind 'e! I got to go town, an' I'm coming back across they tanks; an' Ivy can 'ave wot chap she d'like." Mrs. Strout slammed the door.

Tom rised up and creedled away from village towards the clayworks. He sloojed along, holding one ear, now and then giving un a tug to 'sure hisself that he was awake. He feeled in a sort o' dream and glaazed around the sky in a dazed old manner. Something 'ad been wrong wi' Ivy for weeks - very cool, and allis making excuses for not going out wid'n. He'd been 'fraid they Lobbs had a hand in turning her agin un; the maid would'n say nort when he tried to bring it up, but the neighbours was talking braave 'bout Ivy going to Lobbs' so often.

When Tom got out o' sight o' Pengooth he stepped in be the ditch under a thorn bush, gounjing his teeth, and fooched around the hedge wi' his hand like if he meant to strub a bird's nest. While he was chowing a few bits o' grass he heard somebody call back the road, and squitching round he seed one of his pals, Phin Lorry, knocking along in his corduroys, going to work.

Tom watched un come nearer, and his eyes brightened up, for a idea came to un. When Phin drawed level he stanked from the ditch, spet out the grass and laid hold to un.

"'Ere! Phin!" says he. "You'm goin' work, bean't ee?"

"Where else?" says Phin, glaazen to un braave an' hard.

"An' you do belong washing on the tanks, I b'lieve?"

Phin nodded. "I'm bit early," he says.

Tom pulled at his sleeve so hard that he and Phin both went sprawling back agin the hedge, one on top o' t'other. Tom was the first to git out again, and he sticked hunched in middle the road, poking his head foare.

"Do old man Lobb work wi' 'ee still?" he axed, hoarse in his ussel.

Phin was picking prickles off his trousers, and looking ugly. "No luck itt," he says. "I bin 'oping 'e'd git the sack, but 'e's still there, day arter day, messing around, bossing me about as if 'e was Cap'n."

Tom tugged at his cob. "You bean't very fond of un?"

"I dunnaw nobody wot is."

"I do, wuss luck," says Tom. "Old woman Strout's goin' town d'reckly."

"Well?" says Phin, all taisy. "Wot that got to do wi' Lobb? 'E edd'n goin'."

"She's comin' back across tanks," says Tom, "an' Lobb is goin' help her over some steps somewhere - they'm skittery this weather, an' she'll be snawed under wi' Chrismus traade."

"Well?"

Tom whizzed around 'pon Phin, working his jaw-bones. "You zay you'm early?"

"Iss, I be - abben 'ad no denner wuth much - teddy oggy twas, but

19

mawther spoiled'n - out gabbin' wi' Mrs. 'Icks while ee was burnin' to a cherk. We 'ad a vitty bobsididow about it, an' I catched up me cap an' left 'em. Daresay I'll be down to mykies haaf-hour afore Lobb's there."

"Tha's working jist right," says Tom, and he geeked around all nervy, 'fraid somebody was coming. "I wonder if - could'n ee do zummin?"

"Wot ee want me to do - shove 'em in the tank?" Phin shaaked his head. "Too risky, ole man."

"No, I doan't mane that - no shovin' to be done; only seem me you might manage...... Edd'n ther' a ole board wot Mrs. Strout'd 'ave to stan' 'pon?"

"Iss - arter she'd got up they cement steps ther's a sort o' ladder wi' bit o' planchen on top to walk over afore you git to the path."

"An' wot's in under'n?"

"Water," says Phin.

"Wet? - I mane, dirty?"

"Iss, mucky ole traade, like a lil swamp."

"Deep?"

"Couple feet, praps - anybody'd git stagged up to their knees if they walked in un." He nodded, eyeing Tom uneasy. He seed Tom was purty excited - shaking a bit, and his eyes red as ferrets'. "I c'n zee yer plan," says he. "But I can't risk it. I'd be 'ad up, Tom - running foare an' shovin'...."

Tom rushed foare and shoved un in to the hedge again. "No shovin' to be done, ded'n I tell ee?" he shouted. "Tis zummin else. You'll 'elp me, woan't ee?"

"Oall depends wot you want done," says Phin sulky. "You want to git yer awn back 'pon Lobb an' Strout's woman. I c'n understan' that; I've 'eard wot's 'appening. An' if I c'd vind some way wi'out hurting me awn self...."

"Could'n cut the board s'poase?"

"That would'n do," says Phin, very quick. "They'd zee it, an' would'n tread in 'pon un."

"Edd'n ther' any other board around there wot you might do zummin wi'?"

"Lemme zee - iss, I b'lieve ther' is a plank or two lying along be the path - jist same sort o' planks as wot's put above the ladder, only rotton."

Tom slapped un 'pon the back. "Zackly, zackly," he says, trembling oall over. "Taake up the proper board an' lay down a rotton one - Lobb would'n noatice. Would a break?"

"Who - Lobb?"

"No, the board. You knaw wot a bool ole woman Strout is, an' wi' all her parcels twould be a ton weight 'pon the plonk when she got up. Would a give way, do ee think?"

20

Phin grizzled and made to move on. "No doubt 'bout that," says he. "I'll zee wot c'n be done. Mind, I doan't promise anything. Ther' may be somebody around who'd zee me chaange the planks, but if oall's quiet I'll do me best - tis in between the burras, so nobody would'n be able to spy from roadway."

"Tha's good, ole man," says Tom. "If I c't git they two fam'lies parted an' maake a squabble between Lobbs an' Ivy's mawther, twill be the finest day's work I ever done. I'll be creedling over around 'bout four o'clock - not shawin' meself, o' course - jist to zee wot 'appen. S'long Phin!"

Clocks was striking four when Mrs. Strout got out o' the bus to Trebilcock's corner. She was doodled up braave wi' a gurt old heavy coat and a fur, but twas parcels wot hide her away more'n anything. There was a whacking basket full o' traade to ait, and half-a-dozen big paper bags and boxes wot 'ad presents inside 'em. She had'n bought nort for poor old Tom, but there was a nice scarf for Wilf and a doll for the baby. Mrs. Strout was thinking a pile about they Lobbs, and she reckoned the trick would be done wi' all these presents and Ivy start going wi' Wilf open and stiddy. Old Lobb was worth a heap o' money, and o' course Wilf would git some of it, and twould be a good chance for Ivy. She did'n seem to be red-'ot after un, but be time Christmas was over wi' mistletoe handy and one thing and another, Mrs. Strout believed there'd be a different tale to tell.

She could'n buckle droo so fast as she'd like, and the snaw was come already in lil thin flakes - sky looking awful dark and everything dum and dismal. She was glad when she turned in the short cut - a cart-track leading in off the road half-way up the hill. She'd beginned to pant and squeezed home her eyes to catch sight o' Lobb 'pon the clay tanks. There was a high burra each side of her, and the tanks was gleaming white over t'other end o' the sand. The ground was rough, and she hitched her feet in droaks and nearly went sprawling several times, for she could'n geek around her parcels to see vitty where she was treading. The weight o' the load made Mrs. Strout gasp and puff till of a sudden she stopped short and holla'd out.

"Maaster Lobb! Come ovver 'ere an' 'elp me wi' thaise parcels!"

She glaazed above the box wot the doll was in and heaved a sigh when she seed old Lobb, in his rubber boots, bop up from behind the sluices and come stanking foare to mit her. Big fella he was, clean-shaved, and he grizzled to see Mrs. Strout fooching foare a step or two and then stopping again, all panicky.

"Well, Mrs. Strout," says he when he got close. "Can ee sweat?"

"Purty near," says Mrs. Strout. "I would'n a-b'lieved there was such weight in thaise vew things. If you'll taake the basket, Maaster Lobb...."

"Iss, course," says Lobb, pushing his hand in onder some cardboard boxes and unhitching the basket from Mrst. Strout's numb fingers. "Storm'll break soon, I should'n wonder, but you'll be saafe 'ome in another ten minutes."

They staaved along side be side till they got to the tanks. Phin Lorry was there, over a bit to the left, and did'n seem to take no notice of 'em. Mrs. Strout did'n look at 'e. She kipt chattering to Lobb, and as they went along the tank walls, going slow, she moved behind un, catching hold to his basely old coat and glaazen fearful to the back of his head. Twas braave and skittery, but they never had no mishap, and Mrs. Strout beginned to feel bold as they got to the end o' the tanks, where was a ladder over the marshy place, leading up to the path six feet or so above, what wound to the road close agin Pengooth.

"Now!" says Lobb, stopping short wi' a foot on the ladder. "Lemme 'ave one or two more o' they parcels - I'll lay 'em 'pon the turf up 'ere and then 'ave me 'ands free for helping of 'ee up."

Mrs. Strout hand 'em over and sticked glaazen at the mucky traade in behind the ladder. When she glanced up Lobb was on top the ladder, stanning 'pon a plank wot jutted out over from the path so that the ladder could stand on solid ground.

Lobb stepped down and took her hand, and moving cautious Mrs. Strout went up. Several times her feet slipped, but Lobb had her 'old tight and in a minute he'd stepped back on the planks, drawing Mrs. Strout after un.

"I'm glad - " Mrs. Strout was beginning, when she feeled the board give beneath her, and screeched out: "Aw - !"

Lobb pulled for his life, but twas too late. Under the double weight the plank gived more and more, and afore they could jump back to the path ee'd cracked in the middle, and next minute Mrs. Strout found herself sitting in the plosh, up to her arm-pits in slimy old water, and Lobb, who'd landed on his feet, was floundering around beside the ladder and splattering her face wi' muck.

For a spur Mrs. Strout could'n budge, and then, grabbing hold to the ladder, wot had flopped in agin the hedge, she dragged herself up, plastered all over and streaming wet. Her face was working, and in a minute she'd beginned to rage.

"Wot do ee mane by it, ay?" she screeched. "Wotever maade ee.... You duffan, if I doan't - !"

Lobb spread out his hands apologisin'. His boots was full o' muck, but beyond that he wad'n no worse for his fall.

"Pure accident, Mrs. Strout," says he. "I - I'm some sorry. Would'n for it to 'ave happened for the world. Thikky plank...."

"You must a-knawed ee was rotton! Doan't maake no inscuses! Twas oall den to maake a gaame o' me, you gummock!" She grabbed one o' the pieces o' board and raised it over her head.

"'Ere, 'ere!" says Lobb, all snappy, creedling back to the tank wall. Putt down that board!"

Mrs. Strout reshed at'n, flopping the plank up and down, trying to give un a scat somewhere. "I'll taich ee to fool me agaain - I'll zee!" yelled Mrs. Strout.

Lobb whizzed around sudden and kicked the board out of her hands. Ee went flying down in the mica. Lobb had brindled up now, looking red as a turkey-cock, and boath of 'em was maazed 'nuff to sclow each other's eyes out.

"You woan't never catch me darkening your doors again!" says Mrs. Strout.

"Stay away then!" growled Lobb. "We shaan't be zorry. Wilf bin pestered long 'nuff wi' the maid comin' in so offen. Bin complainin' a lot about it 'e 'ave - caan't injoy 'is new wireless in peace toall for you an' Ivy."

Mrs. Strout stand still, glowing, and clunked like if her breath was took away. She could'n say nort.

While they was sticked there like a couple o' owls Phin stepped up 'pon tank wall and come a bit closer. He 'ad to hold a hand over his mouth to kip hisself from laffin out loud. Things had worked good, and twas plain that Lobb did'n suspect any trick - jist thought that the proper board 'ad broke under the extra weight.

Phin was so took up wi' watching they two that he never noticed a maid coming along the path from churchtown. First he knawed of it was when Ivy spoke perked 'pon edge o' the wall, glaazen down horrified.

"Why, mawther!" the maid cried out. "I come along to help bring in the parcels. Wotever've 'appened?"

Mrs. Strout whizzed around and pointed to Lobb. "That ole booby pulled me up 'pon the rotten plank, and then stamped 'pon un till ee broke."

"You liard!" Lobb spluttered, spitting on his hands. "That there plank...."

"Go 'way an' laive me, or I'll caal the p'lice! Neether me nor you, Ivy, will ever darken their doors agaain. Wilf doan't want ee arter oall, it seem."

"Why should a?" says the maid, cool in a minute. "I'd maade up me mind to break off goin' there - tis maakin' talk, an' Wilf could'n never mane nawthen to me."

Mrs. Strout flounced foare to the ladder, shaking her fist up at the maid.

"You bean't goin' 'ave that penny-liggin Tommy Gumma!"

Tommy hisself heard they words. He was cluffing in one o' the gullies o' the sand-burra, tickled to see how things 'ad shaped out. He

23

waited for the maid's anser wi' his heart scatting quivery.

Glancing around the tanks he seed that Phin had clim'd up the hedge further down than the plosh till he got up on the plat where the maid was stanning. Phin was staling nearer to Ivy.

"Tommy Gumma!" says the maid, and her lips curled sneering. "I shaan't need your 'elp in gittin' me away from 'e."

"Wot!" says Mrs. Strout, glaazen back at Lobb as he sloojed off, and then up at Ivy. "Doan't ee want Tom eether?"

"Nit zackly," says the maid. She turned around. Phin was close to her by this time, and her face lighted up. She smiled to un all sly, and twas plain that they minded some doings what 'ad bin carr'd on behind the scenes for a braave spur.

"Pity mawther an' Lobb is 'ere, Phin," says she, saucy. "These be me old cloas and would'n 'urt if you did git 'em a bit mucky."

Phin wad'n goin' be chated, and in front of 'em all - while Tom rised up in the gully wi' his hands clinched and gounjed his teeth wi' rage - Phin took Ivy in his arms and kissed her.

JOE TONKYN'S VISITORS

For more'n half-a-hour Joe Tonkyn 'ad been there all be hisself in the lodge. 'Pon top o' Goonlerran sand-burra 'twas, on the clayworks, an' the last shift 'ad ended braave while ago. His workmates was gone home an' Joe was left to his awn company, which wad'n terrible cheerful on this pertickler night. Squabbed down on the clayey binch cloase up agin the fire wot he'd kipt burnin', he was thinkin' 'pon the trouble wot 'ad cropped up between he and Jessie Parkyn. The cuddy was cowld, spite o' the fire, an' Joe set hoodled over it, his cap on, pulled down over his eyes to kip his head 'ot. Now an' then he'd glance around the shadowy room - awful bare 'twas, with nort but the two binches in it, runnin' across the long walls opposite each other. He seemed to be all nervy-like, but 'twad'n because he was 'fraid of anybody comin'. He feeled that he was saafe from interruption - nobody would'n traapse to sich lonely plaace, fifty feet up from the roadway, in the cowld an' dark.

That made it all the more startlin' to un when, all of a sudden, there come a knack 'pon the door. He listened fer a tick, hardly believin' his ears. The sound come again; an' this time Joe give a start and squitched around on the sait, glaazin' back. His face was so black as thunder; he feeled maaze to be broke in upon exactly as he wanted it quiet. He though 'twas one o' the workmen an' holla'd out, so taisy as a

25

snaake:

"Wot th' diggens you come for?"

The door opened, somebody stepped in - an Joe gasp, half risin' from the binch. 'Twas a maid, a purty li'l thing in grey coat an' hat - Jessie Parkyn!

For a minute Joe could'n spake 'tall, then he says, clunkin,: "How - how'd *you* git 'ere?"

The maid shet the door and come foare towards un. "I wanted to see ee, Joe," says she. "You knaw that since mawther ferbid us to mit...."

"Ess, ess, I knaw that, my deear maid!" says Joe, all haasty. "I bin thinkin' 'bout et 'ere till I'm cracky, 'moast. Bud I ded'n expeck to see ee in sich plaace a thes. You took the cart-rooad, spoase?"

Jessie nodded. She was smilin' all waik, and her face looked paale in the firelight. Creedlin' foar, she sit down beside Joe 'pon the ferm.

"Yer mawther still howldin' out, Jessie?" says he, glaazin' out droo the winda opposite. Broke 'twas, or one pane of'n, patched up with bit o' rag, and some draught was blawin' in.

"Should'n be 'ere else," answers the maid. She glanced around the lodge, shiverin' scared-like. "Some gashly owld place this es, Joe. Dunnaw 'ow you do stick it."

"Et do main work," says Joe, shakin' his head decisive. "If 'tad'n bin that I'm in work......"

"I knaw. But - but even that - Joe, I wanted to tell ee - " The maid's voice shaaked like if she was nearly squallin'.

Joe seed she had somethin' to tell. He'd got over the shock be this time, mindin' as 'ow Jessie knawed he was gener'ly on the burra for good while arter the others was gone. He rised up from the sait an' stand in frent of her, glowin' down in some pitch.

"Wot is et?" ax he, shouting. "Wot yer mawther got agin me?"

"I caan't think," answers Jessie; "she's 'fraid to trest ee. I dunnaw 'ow, an' I doan't bleeve father's so much agin ee, in the bottom, aunly he doan't like to go agin mawther. But 'tes - 'tes - 'tes droo the work. She say you'm havin' yer spite out on her weth - weth the sand......"

"The - wot?" Joe's eyes was like saucers an' his mouth oppen - comical 'nuff in his face splattered up with clay.

"Sand," says the maid. She motioned Joe to set down again, dabbin' her hand agin the binch right in a gurt splat o' muck wot'd come from his trousers.

"Wipe et off in me jackit," says Joe, holding out his coat-sleeve amoast up agin her noase. Arter she'd rubbed off the wust of it Joe squabbed down gain, couple feet away, nearer the fire. He did'n want her to risk tichin' him an' git her cloas dirty.

"Now, then," says he; "we mus' git to the bottom o' thes. You say there's somethin' you got to tell me - that I be havin' me awn back on yer mawther weth - wot was et?"

"Sand," says the maid.

"Sand," says Joe resolutely, wagging his head to the fire to git the meanin' of it. "Well, wot 'bout that? Tes a maaze to me, Jessie - I caan't see daylight." He lifted his eyes and looked straight out the winda, as if expectin' to see daylight out there. 'Twas all dark, though, ceps for the 'lectric lights shining over the gravelly ridges from some burras li'l way off. And Joe says: "Splain yerself, Jessie."

The maid wriggled on her sait, edging so near to un as she could git wethout muckin' her cloas. "Tes when you do tip," says she then, purty flustered. "You knaw our 'ouze is right in onder the burra 'ere. Well, when tis windy weather nearly oal the sand do git catched as you untip it an' blawed right down our way. We've 'ad et ever since you started trammin' an et do send mawther amoast en sterricks. If the door edd'n kipt shet every mennit o' the day in blaw th' ole gravels an' cover everything - floor an' rugs an' bedcloas - or no, not the bedcloas, cause they'm upstairs, but......"

"P'raps so," says Joe, pullin' up his cap. "But wot that got to do weth me? I bean't the wind."

"I knaw you bean't," says the maid, sympathetic-like. "Ted'n that. Mawther caan't fergit that 'foare you started trammin' we never got a gravel in the plaace. She think you do tip et our way purpose fer spite, an'......"

Joe leaned over the fire and spit. "Yer mawther mus' be dotty," says he. "She knaw very well that 'twad'n till I started workin' here that the traade was tipped that way. They 'ad a extension, Jessie, an' that's 'ow I managed to git the job. 'Twud be the saame now whoever was empt'in' the waggon."

"So I do tell her," answers the maid, beginning to screech. "But she woan't 'ave it to be. She say you do et to aggryvaate her an'......"

"Need'n go tellin' of et oal ovver agaain," says Joe. "Once is 'nuff fer me. Ef the wumman can maake up sich outraageous taale...... But doan't ee go squallin'." He was staring to her like a body stewed. "Ther' mus' be some way out o' thes."

"You'll 'ave to give up yer job," sobs Jessie, wiping away her tears with her clayey fingers and leavin' white spots 'round her eyes.

"I woan't!" answers Joe, gitting to his feet again like a man maazed. He flurrik'd a arm. "No!" says he. "See wot 'twud main. Not a bit o' hope fer us once the job's chucked."

"An' none if you kip un on, onless you can maake mawther bleeve you bean't usin' of'n to git yer awn back. Aw, Joe, 'tes a stank."

"Ess," says Joe, looking sideways across to the grate. "Mus' git up to rights some 'ow." He bend down, geekin' in under the binch. "I'll catch up the vire mennit, Jessie - be 'otter then. There's a stick there be yer foot - tha's of et - hand un here. Thenk'ee!" He plunked the stick in 'mongst the coals and sit down back in his old plaace, 'longside of her.

"Now, 'bout the sand," begins he, very detarmined. "Bean't your party goin' do nort by et?"

"Ess - or laist, I bleeve so. I heeared father tellin' as he was goin' freck up somethin' - a pertition, like......"

"Pertition?" says Joe, glaazin' like a stet. "Wot - indoors? Wot good'll that do?"

Jessie was shakin' her head. "No, nit indoors, Joe. He said he'd fix un up 'pon the garden hadge - maake et lew. He reckoned it'd kip the gravels out, ef he maake un high 'nuff."

Joe was still glaazin', holding abroad one eye with his thumb and finger. "Ded a main et?" ax he, very slaw. "Doan't sim sensible to me. Why, onless he builds hes pertition up half so high's the 'ouze, the sand'll go in ovver the top like ninety."

"No, et woan't," says Jessie, diggin' her shoe in the cracked floor. "Father said the sand do blaw right 'long the top o' the hadge an' if ee was higher ee'd kip it out - laist, moast of et."

Joe chowed it over for a few minutes, winking to the fire, wot was beginning to blaaze away bright again; then he ax, all jerky: "'Ow's a goin' put un up?"

"Drive in staaves, so he said, an' nail up some roofin' traade - somethin' like canvas, I bleeve 'tes. I heeard un tellin' 'bout it."

"'Ave a got the traade?" ax Joe, whizzin' around on the sait some excited.

"He aan't," answers the maid, trying to rub the clay off her eyebrows and maakin' of it wuss'n ever. "An' I dunnaw when he's goin' to. But I've heeard un......"

"That's 'nuff," says Joe, all sharp. He slewed around agaain with his back to her, hoodlin' in over the grate. There was silence for a braave while. Then he wriggled hisself around once more.

"Here!" says he, slappin his knees in some flurrik. "Jessie, I bin an' got it!"

"You knaw wot to do?" ax she, anxious-like.

"Bleeve I got the very thing," says Joe, edging couple inches nearer to her. "Now, your mawther says as I do tip the sand her way purpose to git the plaace lampered with et. Well, if I got the owld stuff fer the pertition an' send it 'long - that'd shaw I wad'n bearin' no maleece in 'eart towards her, would'n et?"

"Ess, Joe - heere!" The maid's eyes shined in under the clayey splats. "Edd'n that grand, Joe? - I bet 'twill do the treck."

Joe was confident. "No doubt 'bout et," says he, spreading his hands out over the fire. "Only I mus' git et quick, afore he do buy et hisself." He raised up all of a sudden and stride towards the door. "I be goin' in Town Saturday," says he; "I'll order it then, an' nex' week I'll send it ovver - or bring et meself; that'd be best, then we could 'splain 'ow the misonderstandin' croped un an'...... But doan't ee braithe a word to nobody, mind."

"I woan't," says the maid - she'd jumped up, so excited as wot he was. "Time fer me to go en now, spoase," says she. "Mus'n rouse no s'picions. You'm laivin' off now, too, bean't ee, when you've maade ev'rything 'ere secure fer the night? Anyway, I'm glad I come up. We can see bit o' daylight now."

"Ess," says Joe, flingin' open the door and glaazin' out to the dark, "we can see daylight now - I'll mind et, doan't you worry."

Few minutes later Jessie was hurrying from the burra down the cart-road, Joe was sticked outside the cuddy lookin' around, and smiling. Other side the burra a man was goin' down droo a gully to the fields belaw - going so fast as his legs would car' un. He was smiling, too - grizzlin' to hisself. He'd heard most o' the talk between Joe and the maid; he'd scoot jist as they raised to go out. He was thinkin' out a plan of his awn.

Next week, sure 'nuff, along come a gurt lorry out to Joe's place and a man stalked in, haalin' a whopping roll o' somethin' wrapped in brown paper. Joe was workin' and his father in bed bad with the 'flu, and so his mawther was fair mystified, cause he had'n said nort to his parents about gittin' the old stuff.

"Thes caan't be fer we," says Mrs. Tonkyn, thinking o' the money wot'd have to be pussed out for it. "We aan't ordered nothin' - some missment maade somewhere."

"No, missus," says the fella, tossing the roll down in the passage and sendin' of it bump into the whatnot. "'Tes ordered en yer sen's naame - an' paid for."

"Aw, is et?" snaps the wumman, glaazin' to the whatnot wot had nearly untipped and was still wobblin'. "An' who towld ee to scat up people's furnisher? Thrawin' the traade aroun' like that......"

"Ee rowled, missus," says the fella, making ready to scoot. He'd catched sight of a rolling-pin in on kitchen table and was 'fraid she'd be taking of'n for un. "I 'polergize ef ee've den any damidge, but...... Good arternoon!"

And 'pon the same the fella run'd out and jumped in the lorry and was gone afore Mrs. Tonkyn knawed vitty wot was happenin'.

Jist 'bout tay-time when Joe come in from work there was some ballyraggin' over thikky roll o' traade. Joe would'n tell wot he wanted it for - only he laid down the law that it mus'n be undone.

"You bean't goin' freck up yer linney, be ee?" ax his mawther as they set foare to the table. Joe had been daggin' for months to put up a linney-place to kip his bike and tools and traade in, but his mother and father would'n consent to it "Cause ef you think you can best us......"

"I doan't," says Joe, very 'umble, winking inside his taycup. "Nawthin' to do weth that," says he. "Thikky rowl o' stuff woan't be 'ere long - nit arter to-morra." He waved his arm, still holding the tay-cup, floxin' some tay out 'pon table-cloth. "No good to ax me any more questions - you woan't git no more out o' me." And with that he banged his cup down with a clatter loud 'nuff to wake half the parish.

Li'l while later, Joe took his big parcel - heavy trade 'twas - and haaled it in the wash-house, up agin the smutty ole boiler. "Be oal right there fer the night," he thought. He could'n car' it over to Jessie's place that evening, 'cause he had to go away on some business for his father, 'bout buying a new pony, and 'tras brave way from his home to Parkyn's, so the job could'n be done afore he set off.

'Bout nine o'clock 'twas when he got back from his bargainin', and he feeled tired out and went in to supper right away, and then straight to bed. He was slaiping in no time - dreaming o' Jessie and his wonderful plan for bringin' everything out satisfyin'.

"Twas pretty dark that night - no moon, and only a few stars shining. There'd been rain and the ground was soft an' heavy, muffling the steps of anybody treadin' over it. Anyhow, Joe was away in the land o' dreams, and would'n have heard the footsteps wot come creedling around 'bout 'leven o'clock. They come 'long the road be'ind and then stopped close to the hedge. Somebody clim'd over and dropped down in the garden. A dim, ghostly shape, carring a big roll o' somethin' wrapped in brown paper. The figure creeped foare to the wash-house and disappeared inside. Few minutes later it came out. It was still carring a big roll......

Joe was that excited over his marv'lous plant that he ded'n notice nothing amiss when he went to the wash-house the next evenin' fer his parcel. Smiling off some proud, he picked up the roll o' trade wot was lying close agin the boiler and walked out to doorway with it, backwards. His mother was there, glaazin' her eyes out.

"Joe," says she, "where be ee goin' car that gurt bundle? Nit far, that's certain - mus' be heavy's lead."

"Et edd'n," says Joe, turning of it 'round the corner o' the path towards frent gate and accidentally poking one end of it agin his mother's noase. "'Tis light as a feather. I must 'ave been overtired last night, I reckon - seemed a lot 'eavier then." And without a fu'ther word off he stanked, hugging his precious roll oke it 'twas a baaby.

Now, there was two ways o' gittin' to the Parkyns' place: around be the road - a long ole jank of it, nearly half-a-mile; and in droo the clayworks, which was a short cut and led out around the sand-burra where Joe belonged workin'.

"I'll taake the cut," says Joe to hisself, and forthwith he clim'd over a stile beside the road li'l way from his home and marched in along a cinder-path, past the clayworks drys and the tanks, 'round the bottoms towards the burra. Stormy evening 'twas, awful cold - some nip in the air and wind 'nuff to blaw away a houze, moast. ' Twas baiting right in Joe's face and he had some job to battle agin it, hampered like he was with the roll. The wind would catch in it all of a sudden and squilch it around, and 'round would go Joe too and run couple yards back towards home 'fore he'd mastered the thing and got hisself to rights again. Puffin' and stewerin' like a steam-engine he was afore he'd got far, the face of him red as a beet, like if he was taisy, which of course he was. And the gravels blawing down from the burra did'n make matters so much better.

'Twas when he got nigh the lew o' the sand-dump that the catastrophe come. Tuggin' to the roll to kip it from being blawed away, he brought one end of it, already bit loose, full force agin a whip o' wind; and in a tick the brown paper 'ad ripped and was flying every way. That wad'n the wust. Next minute Joe was staggering back, and falled down wallop 'pon a heap o' stones wot had rolled down from the burra. Like a maazed man he was glaazin' to the parcel blawin' and dancing' around in frent of him. Now the paper was ripped off he seed wot 'twas he'd brought. *'Twas a roll o' wire-netting!*

Joe had never been so flabbergasted in his life as when he seed thikky traade bouncin' around in the cinder-path. He could understand now why the bundle had seemed so much lighter than 'twas yesterday. But how had it managed to change? Somebody must have stailed his roofin' in the night and left the ole netting in place of it, done up exac'ly same, in brown paper...... The sweat pouring over his chacks, he rised to his feet, limp and shaaky. Some pitiful sight 'twas to see him there, all be hisself in sich wisht place, with the sky comin' in dark and the sand blawin' around, stingin' of'n like hails, his eyes fixed on the bouncing roll. When he stepped foare and grabbed it 'twas with a li'l roar of rage. Somebody'd mained to play a dirty trick 'pon him. Fancy bringing a roll o' wire-nettin' to keep the sand out! Wot would Jessie's mawther 'ave thought o' that? 'Twould be like a insult - only make matters wuss. If he only knawed who......

Suddenly his frame went stiff as a poker. A man was coming around the edge o' the burra from the roadway out other side, where the Parkyns' home was to. Joe squinned home his eyes agin the wind to see who it could be. As the fella got nearer, Joe gasp. 'Twas Tom Parkyn, Jessie's father! Now he was in for it! Fer a minute he had half a mind to scoot, but minded that that would'n be likely to mend things; and anyhow, he was too waik to move far. He jist sticked there, mouth open, waitin'.

Tom Parkyn stride foare, and Joe seed that he was laffin'. When he got close, Parkyn hold out his hand.

"Well, Joe," says he, eyeing the bundle o' netting wot was still whirlin' round like a paper ball; "'ad a accident, sim like."

Joe clunked. He did'n knaw wot to answer. Most likely, Parkyn was laffin' at'n, and Joe'd had 'nuff o' that.

"Better come 'long with me," says Parkyn next minute. "Knaw whose netting' you got there?"

It come to Joe in a flash and he gaaped like a ninny. "Es - es it yours?" ax he, all quavery.

"Ess," answers Tom, grizzlin'. "Caan't see droo et, can ee?"

"Nit yet," says Joe, scratching his head with one hand while he held his cap on with the other. "I spoase - you be maakin' gaame o' me, bean't ee? You've got to hear that......"

"I 'eard everything," says Tom, his eyes twinkling so bright as buttons. "My li'l joke, y'knaw. I folleyed Jessie up burra other night - thought where she was off to - an' 'eard wot you two 'ad to say to each other. Nearly bust me sides, too - fancy Jessie thinkin' I railly mained to freck up roofin' 'pon the headge to kip the sand out! Haw, haw! Why," says he, slapping Joe on the shoulder, "that was jist bit o' fun, teasin' the missus. I knawed she'd got somethin' agin ee - would 'ave it to be you wad'n to be trested, somehow. I never howld for her, but I 'ad to kip quiet or there'd 'ave bin ructions. So when I 'eard......"

"But - but," stammers Joe, panting to the top of his voice, "I doan't see - " He looked sideways to the bundle bouncin down the path.

"My joke again," says Tom, spitting. "When I 'eard you'd railly got the roofin', I thought I'd enjoy a li'l lark. Car'd over a bundle o' wire-nettin' last night an' brought back the roofin'. 'Tis home my plaace now. You mus' come back for et - no good to me. Jessie's waitin' for ee - an' mawther've gived in."

"She - you main - me an' Jessie can go together now oal right?"

"That's of it," says Tom. "When I towld mawther wot you was mainin' to do - buy the traade yerself to kip the sand out - she seed her mistaake in thinkin' you was spiteful towards us. 'Nother thing: I've seed Cap'n, an' he say in few weeks you'll start tippin' lawer side the houze - so everything's oal right. Wait there a tick boy, then we'll be off." And 'way he went jaacin' arter his wire-nettin'.

TEDDY'S TERBOGGIN

"Ernie," says Annie Buzza, stopping short in middle o' Goonvean laane. "I want to tell ee zummin."

"You've towld et oalready, every time we mit, fer the last six months," says Ernie, "an' I bean't tired o' hearin' of et it; so spin away, darlint."

"Aw," says the maid, blushing. 'I wad'n maining that zackly; tes zummin else. What I main es, to begin weth - vather's bad."

"I doan't zee as that be my faut," says Ernie.

"No, ted'n, but twill maake a extra job fer ee, if you'm willin'. He's in bed and woan't be out around fer a braave while, Ernie, 'cording to what doctor an' the weather vorecast do zay." She gived a shiver, glaazen down 'cross to the clayworks what was lighted up with ole 'lectric - cold looking. "Bliv tes comin' snaw, Ernie."

"Look zo, iss, but what's oal this 'bout me doin' zummin fer yer vather, Annie? Caan't yer mawther zee to it, er - er could'n you......?"

"No," says Annie, shaking of her head very slow. "Ted'n no job ver wemmin-foak; tes a man's job, Ernie."

Ernie scratched his nuddik, stamping with both feet like if he was marking time. Twas cold sticked up there, but he mained to git to the bottom o' this afore they went on furder.

"Caan't be gardenin'," says he. "Ted'n time o' year fer that; an' ayven if twas I would'n titch et, Annie. Zee what a gaakin gurt thing yer garden is - big as a gurt turmut vield, an'......"

"Aw, ee edd'n! An' if I tho't you was so lurgy as oal that, Ernie, I'd vinish weth ee, lemme tell ee that, me sen!" She was laffing, and Ernie grizzled too, squeezing of her up to kip hisself 'ot.

"Come on!" says he. "Out weth it! What've I got to do fer yer vather? Tes froozing cowld standin' here, but I woan't budge a inch till I d'knaw."

"Me er mawther would do et, Ernie, in a mennit, and zaave ee the trebble, but - but a red-'ot poker edd'n a purty thing to handle, now is et?"

"Red-'ot poker!" gasp Ernie, glaazen like a stet. "'Ere, 'old 'ard, Annie! Who do ee want me to go clouting?"

"Nobody, you thickhead! Doan't want ee to scat to nort wid'n. Tes fer Teddy's terboggin what he do want."

Ernie falled back a step or two, back agin the hedge; he ded'n knaw toal what she was talking 'bout.

"Like this here," says Annie, laying hold to un and haalin of'n out the ditch. "Teddy got howld of a ole piece o' wood - waaste traade from the clayworks - gurt flat piece 'bout four feet long; an' he want to 'ave et fer a terboggin 'pon the sandburra - to slide on, I main, zetting ascrode. You knaw how the cheldren do play, pullin' their boards up droo the gullies and then skidderin down ovver the side like you do zee 'em in picturs over to forrin parts where there's mountains an' snaw."

"Well! Doan't want to carr' a red-'ot poker, do a? An' ayven if he ded......"

"No, git 'long, Ernie, you'm gittin' proper toatlish. He want to maake a hoale in this 'ere board to putt a stair-rod down droo - that do ack like a brake, you unnerstan', an' when he's goin' too fast Teddy only got to jab the stair-rod down tight in the sand an' that'll stop un. You've zeed 'em do et, abben ee, 'pon the burras there 'longside your plaace?"

"Doan't knaw as I've noaticed," ansers Ernie. He wagged his head. "I zee what you do main," says he; "I got to maake this 'ere hoale. But 'ow musser do et, Annie?"

"You'll zee when you come," snaps Annie. "Teddy want un den right away, so as he can be ready when the snaw come. You mus' toddle over 'morra night, fer sure."

"Oal depends 'pon...... well, I'll come ef I veel like et," says Ernie, rounding up his shoulders. "Laive us git on, maid - tes nipping 'ere. Me veet's like rocks, they be, and me noase es gone slaip, prickin' away like a needle." But 'stead o' moving on he says, savage:

"Still, I doan't zee how yer mawther could'n do et - lil job like that. Nothin' in et, Annie - jist shuv the poker in the vire fer vew mennits, then out wid'n an' putt un droo the board. Aisy as pat."

"Iss, an' aisy to catch ourselfs avire, Ernie - got to 'ave un 'tween our legs, zee - sparks flying every way. We should git our skirts ablaaze ef we wad'n careful."

"An' what 'bout me trousers?" Ernie bust out. He dropped his arm from her and grabbed the knees of his trousers, holding of 'em out in onder his mac. "You doan't worrit 'bout me, whe'er I do git in a mass o' flaames er no. Twould'n maake no deffernce to you if I was burned to the ground."

"Ernie!" the maid cried out, some hurt. "'Ow can ee zay zich things? Whey, ef yer lettle vinger was so much as singed......"

"I was tellin' 'bout me trousers," says Ernie, leaving of 'em go. "Ef ther's sich risk as that you should'n 'ave axed me to do the job - once rewin thaise trousers an' ther's ten bob got to be pussed out be zomebody fer new pair. And twould'n be out o' your pockit. You'm gitting terrible selfish, Annie, tha's what......"

"Now, Ernie, doan't ee go on like that. You do git worked up so quick. You knaw I would'n 'ave ee burn yer trousers, nit fer the world, an' if you hap' to singe 'em, Ernie, I'll buy ee a fresh pair out me awn pockit. There! be veeling better now? I should sclow that there Teddy's eyes out ef we faal'd out over his owld terboggin. You'll be up around 'morra ebenin', woan't ee?"

"Iss, spose," says Ernie, bit sulky still. "Vive o'clock zay - must do it outside and et git dum so quick now in the wenter. Puttin the poker droo taytime, then ee'll be ruddy be time I do 'rive...... But tha's 'nuff 'bout that, Annie - me and you's courtin', I tho't. Laive us talk 'bout zummin else."

Teddy was in some antics over his terboggin: boy here nine year old he was, and bossed the shaw ceps when his father was around; and then, most times, he was 'cross the old man's knee, weth a leather belt goin' over his whatty-call-it.

He renned hom' from school next day and haaled his board out o' the linney where ee'd bin lying 'pon the mucky floor, and come bunking to back door wid'n.

"You bean't goin' bring thikky owld thing in 'ere," says his mother, coming out the doorway to empt' the tay-pot. "Baistly owld thing - ee'd plaster me new carpets."

"New carpets is in the paalour," ansers Teddy. "This wan's goin' in kitchin, an' tha's a stoane vloor wi' nort on un. Bezides board got to be dried fer Ernie to do un fitty. Zo out the way, er yer tay-pot 'll be in sherds!"

And sure 'nuff he stanked in carring his board, and frecked un in frent the vire, lopping up agin the fender.

The dree of 'em never said much droo tay-time. The old man kipt holl'in' down from the baidroom, calling fer more tay or saying he could'n ait what Annie'd carr'd up to un. That was aggravokin' 'nuff, but Mrs. Buzza was taisy 'bout zummin else. She kipt glaazen to the ole board set vore be the stove, and looked 'cross to Teddy like a dagger. He seed she meant to pay un out in some way or other, but he only grizzled, staring to the poker what Annie's sticked in droo the bars o' the vireplace.

Twas brighter weather that day and the dark was holding off nice: Ernie's git the job done, she tho't, afore it come in dum. Then he'd be able to come in and set down be the vire fer a hour - be glad to, she reckoned.

Zo the mail finished and Annie went upstairs fer the old man's dishes. He had'n ait nort to spaik of, and he'd upset his tay, wettin' the baidclo'es. She scoalded un about that, but he only glowed and told her to pull vore the curtains and git the lamp for'n. "An' mind," says he, flurrikin a fist in onder the sheets; "when Ernie come I woan't 'ave no gabbing in 'ere, an' he better not stay long downstairs, eether. I caan't stick it."

"Aw, oal right, vather," says she from the landing. "He'll be so quiet as a mouse if I tell un to mind."

'Fore she got to kitchin vootsteps was heard outside, the gaate clicked, and Ernie stride up the path, whistling. Teddy'd carr'd his board outdoors again while Annie was upstairs and hold un up, shouting out shrill.

"'Ere ee is, Ernie! Good thick board, edd'na? Six inches if ee's haaf-a-foot. Woan't taake long, though, to git the poker droo un - fer you, I main. Twould a-took me hours, spoase."

"Right you be," says Ernie, cheerful; he was glaazen to the door, waiting to see Annie comin'. "Poker 'ot nuff?"

"Iss, reckon," says Teddy, dropping the board with some clatter. "Been hettin' since I come hom' from school. Go 'long in for'n, then we'll 'ave the thing den, Ernie."

Without taking off his 'at Ernie went in. Annie come running fore to un in the passage, her eyes shining.

"En kitchin ee is, Ernie," she told un. "Vather zay you mus'n maake no row - his 'ead is bad and twould maake un split."

"Iss, iss, I'll mind, Annie," says he, lawering his voice. "No noise in a poker - tedd'n like balling in a nail long of a 'ammer. Now, where is a?"

That's what Ernie axed hisself next minute, too, when he stanked in kitchin. He made straight fer the vireplace, but when he got haaf-way fore he stopped short and glaazed. There wad'n no sign of a poker nowhere; the stove door was shet, and the sifter lying in the ash-box all be hisself. He turned to Annie.

"What do this main?" he ax, very quiet.

She was staring with eyes like saucers. "I - I caan't...... Funniest thing I ever seed," she says to herself-like. "When I went up to vather mennit ago that poker was in there" - and she pointed - "red-'ot. Mawther must 'ave......"

But the old woman come bustling in from the pantry, looking awful starn. "Doan't be so fullish, Annie!" she snapped out. "What do ee think I should want weth a red-'ot poker? Lost yer senses, seems to me. I bin en pantry weth the jam and traade we 'ad fer tay."

"Must sarch vor'n tha's oal," Ernie says, gitting taisy. "Licker tis -

36

come in dum soon an'......"

Annie was cluckied down in frent the fender, feeling around inise un. "Could'n a-faal'd out, surely?" says she.

"'Ere, mine yer vingers!" Ernie called out, running fore. "Ef ee's in there and you hap' to titch un......"

"No, ee edd'n in here," ansers Annie, rising. "Edd'n there nowhere. Ded Teddy carr' un out?"

In come Teddy, his faace red and all screwed up. "You knaw I abben had'n," screech he, beginning to dance around with raage. "I 'ad me arms full weth the board." He laid hold to Annie's arm. "Come on now! Where've ee putt'n? You knaw where ee es! Allis playing some prank 'pon me, you lil ole toad! Where's me poker? Tell me where you've heed'n to! Darn'ee, if you doan't I'll scat to ee in the faace an' eyes......"

"'Ere," says Ernie, grabbing the boy's arm. "Doan't you lift a hand to she, me sen, er you'll 'ave me to reckon weth. She doan't knaw where the poker is."

"She do, 'en!" Teddy yelled to the top of his voice.

"Teddy!" the maid bust out. "Think o' vather's 'ead! He'll give you a tannin' when he git better, if you doan't be quiet."

"You've putt 'way me poker! I woan't be quiet till you give un me!"

His mother clout un 'cross the ear. "This 'ave finished the matter, my sen! No terboggin fer you arter this! Ernie can go hom' again, and 'fore he go ther's zummin else he got to do."

"Whassat?" Ernie ax.

"Go out an' saw that board up in lil pieces, so as we can burn un. Saw's in the spence - I'll vetch'n for ee." And she went out in a purty frizz.

Teddy'd beginned to squaal and was struggling to git away from Ernie. "Laive me go! I'll carr' the board off - she shaan't burn un up! I'll vind me poker!"

"Iss, laive us sarch," says Annie. "Ee mus' be here around zomewhere." And down she got 'pon her hands and knees, geekin' in all the corner, in onder the taable, everywhere. Ernie sticked up, glaazen like a man stewed. All sorts o' s'picions was running droo his mind. All of a sudden he give a start and turned 'round.

"Good ebenin', all!" says he, terrible quiet. "Reckon I'll be making tracks."

"Aw no, doan't ee, Ernie!" says the maid, trying to rise up in onder the table and bunking her nuddik. "You knaw what mawther said - here she come weth the saw!"

Ernie raised his voice. "I doan't want none o' yer explanaations, Annie Buzza. I can zee droo et now. Tes oal a treck to git reds o' me - oal the lot of ee 'ave 'greed 'pon this to maake me look like a vool - an' you started et! I o't to a-knawed afore as you was aunly playing weth me. Vancy me clunkin' zich taale as that, b'livin' you wanted me 'ere to 'andle a 'ot poker! Purty lil joke, edd'n et - iss, an' I putt me 'ead in un oal right! But tis yer last." And he stride out, white in the face, and stiff as the poker what he could'n vind.

Ernie belonged tramming zand to the clay-works, 'pon top the burra. Cold job twas now in the winter, and couple days laater the snaw'd come to make it wuss. The burras looked purty in their glistening white coats - like lil mountains; but Ernie went on weth his work jist the same, covering up the snaw with fresh layers o' stone and rubble. He thraw'd hisself in his job like a maaze man - could'n bear to stop and think 'bout what had happened so sudden. He seed it all clear 'nuff: Annie had'n railly wanted'n, and Teddy's terboggin had put her in mind of a way to shame Ernie afore all her family so that he'd never shaw his faace in frent of 'em again. A wicket lil plan that was, and Ernie's blid boiled to think he'd bin so aisy drawed into it and made a laughing-stock of hisself. O' course, she'd hide the poker, and then made outs...... Twad'n no odds, though now. Everything was finished between 'em and he would try an' vind zomebody else.

Come Saturday he started his day's work as usual. 'Bout ten o'clock, when he got out to tip with another load he 'ad a bit of a shock. He could see the Buzza's home from here - not far off - jist 'cross a vew fields; but there wad'n nobody outside fer un to look at.

Twas closer at hand: zummin moving fu'ther down - lil dark smudge agin the white snaw and sand. Fer a mennit he could'n maake out zackly what twas, and then it come to un, a fitty stunner. Teddy Buzza, and on his terboggin, skidderin over the rough slope like a flash. He jist glaazed till Teddy got to bottom, then shouted like a witnick.

"Git out the way, you idjit! I got to tip, an' you'll 'ave thaise stoanes 'pon top of ee ef you doan't scoot off. Go on now, do ee hear?"

Teddy squitched around and glaazed up. Ernie seed the lil faace long way belaw - lil red blob; an' next minute Teddy waaved to un.

"Git out the way!" shouts Ernie again. "You young ninny - do ee want to 'ave yer head cut abroad?"

"Down 'ere!"

"Ay?"

"Come down 'ere, I zay! Ren down 'ere!"

"Whaffor?"

"Got zummin to tell ee!"

Ernie laid hold to the wagon. "Look! 'Ow many more times...... You'll be killed! I'm goin' tip the waggon."

"Twad'n no good. Teddy'd left his terboggin and started to clim' up the burra, in one o' the ruts. Ernie waited, veeling maaze, while the boy come nearer. Vew mennits, and they was faace to faace.

"Well!" Ernie rapped, poking out his chin. "Wha's oal this 'bout?"

"I got me terboggin den," says Teddy.

"Doan't want to hear nothing 'bout no terboggin," Ernie told'n.

"I den un meself," Teddy went on, some proud. "While mawther was off to town yes'day. I ded'n think I could manage et - ted'n den proper, I spoase, like you could a-done it. Still, do work oal right."

"What do ee want to tell me, then! I caan't waaste time 'ere."

"'Bout thikky poker" - Teddy grizzled. "Knaw who den it?"

"I do knaw," says Ernie, very bitter. "That there maid......"

"No maid toal," says the boy. "Shall I tell ee?"

"No harm, spoase." But Ernie's off-hand way o' spaking could'n hide the fact that he was purty aiger to hear more 'bout it.

"Twas like this," says Teddy. "Tay-time there, I bro't in me board to dry in frent the vire. Mawther was vexed over it an' 'tarmined to git her awn back; so while I was carring the board out, an' while Annie was up vetching vather's tay-things, mawther whipped the poker from vireplace an' carr'd un in pantry."

"Ernie was braithing hard, lying back agin the truck all weak. "'Ow - 'ow ded ee vind out?" he ax, clunking.

"Saame ebenin'," Teddy went on, scrabbling up some snaw and making a ball of it, "I went in pantry fer clunk o' watter. I dipped me cup in the putcher and drinked off - but lor, I soon spewed et out agaain."

"Howzat? You main - she putt the poker - in the putcher?"

"Iss. Put un in the putcher. Tha's what she done. And so it oal come out." He haived the snawball out over the burra, watching of'n tumble droo the air and vall hundred veet belaw. "Maid's in some stew," he says then. "Squaalin' oal last ebenin', an' abben spok' to mawther fer two days. Be goin' patch it up, er no?"

Ernie was glaazen 'cross to the Buzzas' house. Oal to once he zeed Annie come out and creedle up the back garden path - no spirits in her - just sloojing on.

"Annie!" he yelled sudden, fair busting his lungs.

She stopped like a body shet, looked up.

Ernie blawed her a kiss.

And coming to life again quick, she blawed back two!

PERCE TREZIDDER'S REVENGE

Twas a queer sight, and Freddie Neale stopped short for a minute to Goonamarris corner, glaazin'. Though twas braave and late, and a dark night, he seed very dim that something unusual was happening in frunt of un. Fore by the house opposite, outside gate, a man's form was shuffling and dancing around, not making no noise ceps now and then a funny old grating sound, like a stone moving. The figure kipt ducking and pulling at somethin', goin' round and round - awful queer, and Freddie was nigh scared for a tick or two. Then he braced hisself up and moved on, scatting his feet loud along the road to let the fella knaw he was comin'.

Be time he got close the fella was standing up by the gate, very stiff. Freddie seed that he'd took off his boots and set 'em be the wall. He reco'nized un right away - twas Perce Trezidder from Nanpean.

"Why, Perce!" says Freddie. "Wot be doin' of?"

"Nothin' much." Perce hold up his hand, leaned back agin the wall and glaazed about, cool as a cucumber, as if he had'n never titched nort what belonged to other people.

"I seed ee doin' zummin' ere," says Freddie, poking out his chin.

"Could'n 'ave," says Perce, spaking under his voice. "Zummin' took me jist mennit, as I was comin' round the corner - veeled oal giddy, an' I nearly falled 'long the road. I come fore 'ere to hold on to the gaate-poss till it passed."

"No sich thing! I seed ee cluffin' over this 'ere stoane, goin' round an' round an' tuggin' away like if......"

Perce stepped fore and grabbed Freddie's arm. "Zay that again!" says he, terrible quiet, and he shaked his fist close up agin Freddie's noase.

"Well, p'raps I was mistook," gasped Freddie, very 'fraid. "Twas dark, I knaw, but I tho't......"

Perce shuvv'd un away. "Go 'ome!" says he. "Do ee hear?" Git along, afore I knack the breff out of ee!"

"But wot be on 'pon? I woan't tell nobody, Perce, aunly ther's zummin' doin' 'ere wot no business to be. May not be your faut......"

"Go 'ome!"

Freddie come near again and cluffed over the stone out-side gate. He laid hold to un and found that the thing was loose and haff out o' the hole. Perce stepped fore and gived un a push, and Freddie went back in the road and sit down more quick than comfortable. He striggled up but still he ded'n move off. And of a sudden Perce changed his mind.

"May as well tell ee," he says, whispering, and beckoned Freddie over to un. "Aunly you muss'n laive it go no further."

"I woan't," Freddie promised, and he stanked fore, treading 'pon his toes, and set down on the stoane.

"Well," Perce went on, stooping and whisperin' in his ear. "I'm goin' to carr' off this 'ere old stoane o' Giles's - tha's wot I'm doin' of. They'm oal gone to slaip be this time, an' 'morra mornin' they'll 'ave a shock - nothin' to swing their gaate back agin."

"But - wotever 'ave tooked ee, doin' sich thing as that? Tedd'n saafe, Perce - zay if twas bobby 'stead o' me wot come round the cornder."

"I 'ad to chance that," says Perce. "Got to 'ave me spite out on 'em zome 'ow. Ded'n dare go inzide gaate to carr' off anything - they might a'heard me. This 'ere owld stoane is oal that was 'andy, zo off he's goin'."

"Wot be goin' do wid'n, Perce - gurt owld stoane like that?"

"No odds to you," snaps Perce. "That's me awn sacret. Bean't goin' tell you everything."

Freddie sniffed. "But wot 'ave 'em done to ee?"

Perce stand upright and shaked his fist towards the winda. "They bin talkin' 'bout me," says he, hoa'se in his ussel.

"Anything very bad?" ax Freddie.

Perce forgot hisself and shouted out sudden: "Bad 'nuff! Been zayin' I'm runnin' arter Job's maid. Old scare-craw! You knaw her, doan't ee - Mattie Job?"

Freddie nodded, shifting on the stone. "Ess," he says, some quiet. "Nort very wrong in zayin' you looked at she, is there? I wouldn' fly in no temper if anybody said I'd seed her. Purty maid, I think - very purty maid."

"G'at! You dunnaw a purty maid from a paycock! Go round like that she do - oal frills an' feathers. An' they bin zayin' I mit her."

"Zo you did, I bet."

Perce stamped 'pon the ground in his stockings, right on a sharp bit o' rubble, and went red in the face. "Look 'ere!" he spluttered. "Twas a accident - pure accident, Freddie, tha's oal twas."

"Wot - that you was vound out?"

"No; twas a accident that I was on the bus saame sait as she t'other day. Owld woman Giles happened to zee it, an' spread a taale - oal lies! They knaw tis lies, too, an' - an' - an'......"

Freddie waggled his fingers. "'Ush!" says he. "They'll 'ear ee ef you doan't mind. Wisht job for ee then."

Perce bit his tongue; he'd got worked up to his pitch and geeked fust one way and then another, desperate.

"Wot ded I tell ee?" he snapped in a whisper. "Go 'ome!"

Freddie rise up very slow. "Good-night, Perce!" says he, and creedled off. It is had'n been so dark Perce might a-seed un wink to hisself.

Early next mornin' there was some fluster outzide Giles's place. Old Giles, goin' down to tap for water, had noticed the stone gone and holla'd out to the women, and soon the dree of 'em was frecked around the hole, glaazin' to each other proper stewed.

"Zomebody been 'ere in the night," says Giles, bawling in his wife's ear - bit deaf she was.

Their darter, Sarah, looked at un and slapped her hand together. "I b'leeve I knaw who done it," says she, screwing up her lil mouth tight.

Her father cocked his eyebrows, blinking. "Who do ee reckon twas, Sarah?"

"Freddie Neale," says she. "He bin riled 'cause I woan't look at un, an' I bin expectin' zummin'."

"So've I," Mrs. Giles broke in, all gaspy. "I've allis said that old Perce bean't to be trested."

"Mawther!" screeched the maid, laying hold to her arm and shaking of her. "We said Freddie Neale, nit Perce!"

"Course I did!" says the old woman, glaazin' to Sarah some taisy. "I seed un with her, there in the bus."

"Tes Freddie! Freddie Neale! Aw faather, she caan't 'ear wot we'm zayin'. You think tes Perce done this, mawther?"

"No, not once, but tedd'n no good for un to deny nort they was seed together."

Sarah laffed nervous. "Be that as may," she snapped, turning to old Giles, "you party no business to make sich a fuss about et. Everybody think Perce wanted to go courtin' wi' Job's maid an' that she would'n taake on wid'n - maade Perce a laffin'-stock it 'ave."

Mrs. Giles stepped fore quick, not looking where she was goin', and if Sarah had'n grabbed hold to her she'd a-tumbled in the hole.

"I tell ee I seed un settin' beside her in the bus," she shouted out when she got her balance. "He was leanin' close to her an' whisperin', an' I bleeve he 'ad his arm round her neck. That mus' main zummin."

"No, he ded'n!" ansers Sarah at the top of her voice. "You'm short-sighted an' you seed double. Perce would'n put his arm round no maid's neck - I knaw he would'n. He edd'n that sort."

"Aw," old Giles grunted, eyeing her some close. "Purty aiger to taake sides wi' Perce, bean't ee? Want un to put his arm round your neck, s'poase?"

"No, I doan't!" she snapped, waving her arms in a proper flurrik. "But Perce never carr'd off thes stoane. Zay wot you like - twad'n Perce, twas Freddie."

"Tha's right," says Mrs. Giles, mumblin'. "But if we'd aunly bin ready afore...... I'd a-bin ready for'n wi' the rollin'-pin. I never ded like Perce."

The ring of a bike bell sounded afore Sarah could anser, and next

minute the man 'ad come round the corner. Soon's he seed 'em he pulled up and jumped off, stepping in by the ditch. Twas Tom Neale, Freddie's father.

"Knaw who done this?" he ax right away, clappin' a hand over his mouth to save hisself from grizzlin'.

"We was tryin' to guess," says Giles, looking very starn. "Twad'n you, was et?"

"'Ardly," says Neale, chuckling. "But I can clear it up for ee, I bleeve. Freddie come 'ome last night sayin' he'd seed Perce Trezidder outzide 'ere pullin' up the stoane. An' that edd'n goin' be the end of et. Freddie said Perce is comin' again to-night an' do zummin wi' the stoane. Should'n be s'prised ef he ded'n smash yer windas. In some taare he is 'cause o' wot you been tellin' 'bout he an' Mattie Job."

"Ess, good job you 'ave," says Mrs. Giles, holding a hand up behind her ear. "Tha's only thing wot'll stop un."

Giles whistled, but he ded'n look as if he believed wot Neale 'ad tole 'em. "We'll 'ave to zee the p'lice 'bout this," he says. "Git bobby 'ere to-night."

"Should if I was you. No knawin' wot Perce'll be doin' else - he doan't care fer nawthen ner nobody."

Sarah drawed herself up stiff, and curled her mouth all sneering. "You better tell Freddie 'bout it, er he may git nabbed," she flashed out.

Neale give a jump and kicked around the pedal of his bike some vicious. "Freddie! Wot! You doan't think twas he......"

"I bean't zaying," ansers the maid, goin' backwards up the steps. "But a warnin' woan't do un no harm, well et?"

Next minute Neale was gone and Giles stanking down the road towards Foxhole village to tell the p'liceman.

That night there was a bit of a moon, but twas nippin' cold, and the man creedling along the road droo Goonamarris carring a ladder over his shoulder kipt shivering, glancing about uneasy.

When he got to the corner he stopped, tossed the ladder over the hadge and clim'd up arter un, and dropped down in the field. Close by, heed away 'mongs some brembles, was a white flat stone - the one wot 'ad been pulled up from Giles's gateway the night afore.

Perce grizzled as he took un up, tucked un under his arm - twad'n a very 'eavy stone - and holding the ladder low down he tread quiet along by the hadge till he got opposite Giles's housen. Quiet and cautious he geeked over the hadge. Nobody to be seed. The wind was whistling braave, and a pail outside the Giles's wash-house was blawing to and fraw, rattling on the cement. That'd cover his movements - nobody would'n hear un.

There was a gateway to the field, but no gate in un, and soon Perce 'ad stride out droo, crossed the road, and clim'd the garden hadge. He was then to the back o' the dwellin'-place, and feeled scared for a croom. Then his teeth grit, and he dropped the ladder and the stone in the path, cluffed down and stripped off his boots. No sound did'n come from the bedrooms, all was dark inside and Perce beginned to git reckless. Anything to 'ave his awn back! They old Gileses was playin' wreck with his life, spreading sich tale. Twas trew he'd bee on the bus wi' Mattie Job, but it did'n mean nothin; he'd never cared tuppence about that maid. Twas somebody else he'd got crazy about, and they tales kipt un off from her. That was why Perce was so spiteful.

He set the ladder leaning agin the eaves - tricky old job, but Perce was used to handlin' ladders and managed it purty well in the moonlight. Then, holding his stone under one arm, he beginned to clim' up. His stockings never made a sound 'pon the rungs, but he feeled all quivery as he got above the bedroom winda. If anybody should hap' to wake now - or zay they'd been watchin' for'n! Lor massy, wot would a do? But he nerved hisself to go on, and soon he was on the roof.

Twas foozin' cold 'ere, and the wind scattin' right in his eyes. The slates wad'n easy to clim' over, but dropping to his knees he crawled up the roof towards the chimney-pot, huggin' the stone. The moon shined on un, and with his coat flapping round un like a gurt black wing he looked very queer - some funny old bird, you might a-thought.

Reaching the chimley-pot Perce stopped and glaazed about. The ground was so far belaw that he gasped and feeled giddy for a tick. Then, grabbed hold to the chimley he rised slowly to his feet and laid the stone 'cross the top o' the pot, coverin' up the hole.

Zackly as he'd got un fixed a sound come from down under - the bedroom winda opening! He ducked quick and sit still as a mouse, holding his breath, glaazin' with eyes like bools to the bottom o' the roof.

Somebody was whisperin': "Perce! is et you?"

He did'n anser for a braave while, but at last he says, some hoa'se and quaavery: "Ess."

"You owld zilly!" says the maid. "Wot be doin' of up there?"

Perce beginned to skidder down the roof. "Aw, I - I mended yer chimley-pot. I main, I......"

"Giss on! Ee wad'n broke. I knaw wot you bin doin', an' I knaw why. Twill be oal right, Perce - need'n a-got in sich a frizz about et."

She 'eard Perce panting up over the eaves, and then he says gulpy: "Bout wot?"

"My people gabbin'. I veeled mawther must a-put the wrong sense to it. I knawed 'ow you veeled - I've noaticed 'ow you've looked at me several times, an' - well, tis up to you, if you want anything to 'appen."

Perce cluckied down 'pon the roof, shaking all over and white as a sheet. "Wait a mennit!" he gasp. "Lemme git 'pon the ladder." He stretched his hands out to the ladder, wobblin' so much that Sarah give a cry, 'fraid he was goin' to fall. But arter a minute he got safe on the rungs and beginned stepping down, and soon he was level with her, lying flat on the ladder, his face pushed in between the rungs. He lied there gaspin' so long that the maid drawed back frightened; his eyes was fair popping out, and he'd nearly knacked his cap off. But presently he stammered zummin like this:

"You main - you - you'm sweet on me, be ee?"

"Tedd'n fer me to zay," ansers Sarah, some sly, "till you've lemme knaw if tis any good. I bean't goin' waaste words."

Perce haived hisself back a bit, and his cap falled off, went splash down in a pool in the gutter. "Aw, drat et!" he snapped, and turned to the maid. "Well, you knaw oalready - o't to, anyway. I bin cracked about ee - tha's why I done oal this. I was maaze to think your party 'ad turned ee agin me."

"The abben," says she, coming close again. "Nobody could'n do that, Perce. You carr'd off the stoane - ded ee?"

"Ess."

"An' wot've ee den to the roof?"

"Stopped up yer chimley-pot," says Perce, looking some 'shamed of hisself. "Twould a-buried ee down wi' smok' an' smuts to-morra. I'm zorry - I'll go up an' taake un off in a mennit, an' woan't never do no sich things no more. Do ee forgive me, Sarah?"

He poked his head in between the rungs again, and the maid craaned her neck to git her face out titchin'.

Down in the road a bobby come stealthy to the garden hadge and glaazed up. He'd been meaning to catch Perce red-'anded, catch un in the act, and so 'ave proof o' what he mained to do. He seed the flat stone resting 'pon chimley-pot and feeled he was in for a aisy job.

The bobby blinked and could'n hardly bleeve his eyes. Up there be bedroom winda two people was kissin'. Perce was trying to git his arms to stretch far 'nuff round the ladder to hug the maid standing in bedroom. He ded'n manage it, but bobby 'eard un say somethin' 'bout "morra night" and drawed his own conclusions. He feeled there wad'n nothin' for un to do, so he creedled away with a grunt and left 'em.

NOAH'S TORTOISE

Twas nipping cold, three days afore Christmas, and up here 'pon St. Dennis Downs there was some wind blowing; but that ded'n matter much to the couple what I'm goin' to tell 'ee about - Mary Barkla an' Dick Rawe. They had other things to worry 'em more'n the weather - though o' course, while they was out wi' one another they ded'n worry at all. They'd slipped in between the sand-burras be a old inyun-house and was sheltering where twas lew, in the doorway. Mary gave a lil giggle, snuggling up close to Dick.

"There'd be ructions if gran'fer knawed I was up 'ere wi' you agaain," she says.

"I knaw," says the chap - good-looking chap he was, though it could'n be seed now, cause twas dark; and he frowned down towards St. Dennis, seeing in his mind a old fogey of a man with whiskers, what was the only relation Mary had left. "Caan't ee dor nort by et, maid?"

"No; I've tried an' tried, but he woan't lissen. 'E an' yer father abben bin on spakin' terms fer 'ears - neether wan of 'em woan't maake et up. I doan't bleeve 'e'll ever cunsent, though I'm oal 'e got in the worl' to look arter un an' you'd think 'e'd be more sinsible fer his awn saake."

"Bit shaaky, is a?"

"Ess, 'e edd'n too braave - catched a cold; but 'e's that pig-'eaded 'e woan't stay indoors. 'E'll 'ave a relapse an' be back in bed afore long, you zee. Tis a purty Chris'mus I sh'll 'ave of it, a-tendin' to granfer."

Dick sighed deep and shaked his head mystified. "I caan't see toal why 'e sh'd stand out agin me - clane, 'ard-workin' chap like I be. Wot 'arm 'ave I done? An' doan't a ever think 'bout you - selfish ole thickhead!"

"'E knaw it do maake me miserable," says the maid, "but 'e doan't care. I bleeve 'e do love 'is ole tortiss more'n 'e do like me. Allis talkin' 'bout the ole tortiss 'e is, ever since 'e had'n back in the spring."

Dick broke off a stub o' grass from beside the doorway and chowed it for a minute. The wind reshed past, scattin' gravels like hail and making some racket round the roof o' the inyun-house. Dick hold the maid tight, and she was beginning to wonder what he was thinking when he says very thoughtful:

"You say 'e do love this 'ere tortiss?"

"Ess - more'n 'e do like me I said, an' I bleeve tis trew."

"An you reckon 'e's goin' be bad in bed for Chris'mus?"

"Moast likely, if 'e d' kip goin' outdoors this weather. But wot that got to do wi' it?"

"I jist tho't," says Dick. "I bleeve I got a idea." He cleared his throat and spit, then stooped and whispered for several minutes in the maid's ear.

"Dick!" she says excited when he'd finished, and she give un a smacker. "You've 'it et!" We'll be doin' this in onder the misletoe in granfer's awn paalour afore the New Year - zee if we woan't!"

Next morning Noah Crowle was leaning over his front gate down village when Tubby Lobb come along the road from Enniscaven.

"Well, Noah," says Tubby, his fat red face shining off in the sunshine. "Ow's it goin'?"

"Wisht, wisht," Noah pants out. "I do git so tight 'ere - caan't braithy." He tapped his chest. "Brownchitis, Maaster Lobb."

"So I've 'eard. Should think you o't to stop indoors."

"Huh!" Noah grunted, jerking a thumb back to the kitchen winda. "You caan't knaw much o' women's comp'ny. If you 'ad a gran-darter like I got you'd be glad to git outside, rain er snaw, 'ot er frewze, you would."

"Aw," says Lobb, glaazen uneasy up to the sky. "Well, p'raps I'd best not mention her. 'Ow's yer turkle?"

He thought this would put Noah in better humour, but instead the old man' face went like a beetroot.

"Turkle! Tedd'n no turkle toal - tes a tortiss."

"Saame thing," says Lobb.

"Tedd'n saame thing toal - turkles is gurt big animals, like gurt elephants compared to a tortiss."

"Ow do you knaw? You never seed a turkle."

"I've seed pictures o' turkles," roared Noah, shaking the gate and making as if he would stride out and scat Tubby flat in the road. "Turkles wi' cheldern a-ridin' 'pon 'em like hoss-back. Wot I got is a tortiss, an' doan't you go insulkin' me again."

"Well, 'ow is a?"

"'Ow can I knaw? Ee bin slaipin' fer months in me back garden, an' ee'll be there for six months, out o' sight."

"Ee mus' be dead be this time," says Lobb, who liked teasin' the old man. "No animal alive could'n live six feet in onder the ground."

"Who said ee was six feet in oner the ground?" Noah bust out. "I said ee'd slaip fer six months, nit six feet."

"Aw, six months, was et? Well, any'ow, I'd dig un up if I was you an maake sure ee's still alife. Tedd'n the right way to treat no pets, a-buryin' of 'em up oal winter. Who'd think o' puttin' a cat......"

"Me tortiss edd'n no cat no more'n tis a turkle," snapped Noah, fairly dancin' on the steps. "I knaw 'ow to look arter mun. I've reed it up in books, an' tha's more'n you 'ave. An' twad'n me wot put'n under-ground - ee buried hisself up. Come up garden an' zee if you doan't bleeve me."

Noah flinged open the gate. Tubby tread in, grizzling to hisself, for

48

he liked to pull Noah's leg a bit and git his hair in a knot. Noah stanked around the house corner, wheezing braave, and fooched up garden path. Near the top, where some rhubarb was planted, was a square space o' earth, marked around wi' stones brought down from the sand-burra; and between the stones a gurt post had been frecked in the ground wi' a board nailed on top of un.

When they got close Tubby stopped short and glaazed to the board. There was gurt capital letters on un, done in white paint, high 'nuff to be read by anybody passin' 'long the road. And it went like this:

"WARNING:
LIVE TORTOISE BURIED HERE
ANYONE TRAMPLING WILL BE PERSECUTED.
NO STONES TO BE THROWN."

Lobb glanced back to Noah s'castic. "Who do ee think's goin' clim' the hadge an' traapse 'cross yer garden?" he says.

"There's no knawin'," answers Noah, trying to bite his whiskers. "People got ways with 'em."

"But if you ded'n put up the noatice they would'n knaw 'e was there. Tis axin' fer trouble, that is."

Noah clinched his hands. "I'd like to zee the man who'd try to up-root me tortiss," he says vicious, and he poked his head fore so far that Tubby drawed back and squat down 'pon the hedge.

"Wot do ee main, Noah," he ax, pointing to the board again: "'No stones to be thrown'? Could'n tich the turk - tortiss I mean."

"Might waake mun up," says Noah, bending down two-double and geeking around s'picious-like. "Twould be the death of un. I do alw'ys tread soft past 'ere, minding 'ow close ee is - an' I doan't gab loud neether, as you can see." And indeed, though twas easy to see Noah was fitty riled, he was spaking uncommon quiet.

Tubby laffed scoffing. "Wonder you doan't put yer ear down an hark to hear'n snorin'," he says.

"G'at! Tortisses doan't snore. You'm a hignorant man you be, an' doan't knaw nothing." Noah coughed; his wheeze was gittin' wuss, and he give a shiver. "I mus' be goin' in. Tis too cowld fer me up 'ere. I'll be laid up if I doan't mind." His skinny arm shoot out towards Lobb as he beginned hobbling down the path.

"Oal your fault - wantin' me to come up 'ere in this wind an' shaw ee where me tortiss is! I was then goin' in be the vire when you come along."

"Zorry," says Lobb, very 'umble. "I speck twill pass off soon's you git in an' het yerself."

But it ded'n prove so. Noah was soon fitty out o' sorts. He'd lost his

49

50

appytite by tay-time and set wheezing away over his cup and plate, glowin' across the table to·where Mary was eating Chris'mus caake and trying not to look guilty. Next day he had a braave sweat and could'n leave the house. On towards night - Chris'mus Eve twas - he got wuss, all shivery, wi' aches and pains, and kipt snapping at the maid, wanting this and that brought to un.

"Bleeve I got the 'flu," he groaned, rolling round in the big chair, his eyes glaring red. "All your doin's - drivin' me outdoors weather like this! Want to git reds o' me you do."

Mary was bustling too and fraw, laying the lil round table wi' Chris'mus traade, nuts and sweets and fruit, and putting a fresh stick or two on the fire. She glanced wistful now and then up to the beams and round the walls - some holly frecked up there, but no mistletoe itt. She'd put that away in a drawer, and twould only come out jist afore Dick come in - if he ever did.

Noah rised threatening; he could'n shout, he'd near lost his voice, but twas some awful sound what come gasping out.

"Doan't you dare mention 'is naame in this 'ouse! Dick Rawe shall not be spoke of 'ere while I got breff......"

But Noah found he never had nuff breath to finish, and flopped back in the chair, scrabbling at his waistcoat, and did'n said another word till he was safe tucked up in bed.

Noah was snoring like a top afore he'd bin to roost long, and Mary smiled to herself, listening to bottom o' the stairs. Granfer was slaiping right 'nuff - he would'n be likely to wake for a hour or two. Having made out the lamp she tread very quiet back to door and put on her hat and mac. Opening the door without any noise she stepped out.

Twas lovely moonlight now, clear sky, with a bit o' frost but no wind to speak of, and Mary's heart feeled light as she creedled down to gate, out in the road and off towards the downses. She didn't dare go droo the village where she might be seed and took a roundabout way in across some fields from Hendra. Soon she'd got to a claywork and made along a cinder path in the shada of a sand-burra below 'Starrick, where Dick had 'greed to mit her if all was well. Sure 'nuff when she got half-way over the downs above Bodella Farm, there was Dick shivering in onder a thorn-bush, looking some anxious. But when he catched sight of her face he gived a sort o' jump and come running fore and grabbed hold to her proper style.

"Zo things is workin' out fitty - be 'em?"

"Cound'n be better," says the maid - "that is, if you done your part oal right."

"I done my part, doan't you fret," says Dick. "You'll zee d'reckly. Ther' woan't be no danger o' waakin of'n up, will ther'?"

"Not now 'e got the 'flu - 'e'll slaip like a ringer, an' do snore so loud 'e would'n 'ear no other sound even if 'e waked up."

Dick laffed. "Now you'm talkin' silly," he says. "But I knaw wot you main. 'E'll be up bed oal day 'morra, woan't a?"

"Ess - I'll 'ave to zend fer doctor, I s'poase. Some ole job. But that woan't matter so long as you can come over in the evenin' an' set down wi' me in paalour. Twill be like a merricle."

Dick agreed twould. "But will 'ee want any 'elp? he says. "Tis a job wot'll need careful handlin', an' maids bean't allis to be trested. I main," he added quick as Mary duffed his nuddick, "I main they d'do too good a job an' spoil everything."

"I'll manage oal right on me awn," says Mary. "Come over early 'morra mornin' - eight o'clock zay - an' if everything 'ave gone well I'll be waavin' to 'ee from back garden. Else I'll be indoors, an' you'll 'ave to go 'ome again."

"I could'n bear et," groaned Dick, holding his head desperate. "Twould main another year o' this 'ere - gittin' of us nowhere. You mus' stick to yer guns, Mary, an' not give in, laive un shout the 'ouse down."

"I woan't," says Mary. "'E'll give in oal right when 'e find 'ow we got'n cornered. An' now I mus' slip 'ome again - if 'e should waake up an' find me gone twould knack everything. Tis 'morra we'm 'avin' our courtin' night, Dick - in Granfer's awn paalour!"

"I 'ope so," says Dick, and for a braave spur he seemed to think the thorn-bush was mistletoe!

When Noah waked up on Chris'mus morning he found Mary in the bedroom smiling to un as if she had a secret what she was daggin' to tell.

"You 'ere!" snapped Noah. "I've 'ad a wisht night. I'm sweatin'. I want some drink."

"In a mennit, granfer - I've light the fire. But I tho't I'd 'ave zummin rail Chris'mussy fust - 'long. You abben give me nothin', but I doan't bear no malice, and I bin plannin' zummin for 'ee. Sit up an' look!"

Noah striggled up on a elbaw and glaazed round the bed. Wad'n no stocking there padded out, nor nort else what he could see, more'n the cloas what belonged there.

"Wha's thes?" he ax, all taisy.

"Santy Claus bin, granfer - look wot 'e bro't 'ee! Down 'ere 'pon the floor, look!" And she stepped aside so Noah could see right across the room.

Noah blinked out droo the bedrails and seed to once that somethin' was down on the carpet, a greyish round sort o' thing what was moving very slow towards the doorway.

"Wotever......! I mus' be dreamin'," says Noah, rubbing his eyes and leaning fore in bed to glaaze at the objick.

"No, no, you bean't dreamin', granfer," says the maid, soothing. "Nice su'prise for 'ee, edd'n et?"

But Noah had flinged the bedcloas right and left with a screech. "Me tortiss! Me tortiss! 'Ow did ee git up in me bedroom?"

"I bro't un in, granfer - tho't twould cheer 'ee up to zee yer lil pet again. You abben seed un fer so long. Sh'll I put un up on the bed for 'ee to cuddle?"

Noah bounced up and down like a maazed man, thumping his hands together. "You idjit! Caan't 'ee zee wot you've done? You've murdered that tortiss! Taake un out an' bury un this mennit - 'ee'll die in 'ere. O't to be left slaipin' six months in that garden. I'll carr'n out mesself -!" Noah got one leg out over the side of the bed. Mary raised her hands quick and waved un back, looking a bit frightened.

"No, no doan't go over an' titch un, granfer. Tis 'ot in 'ere an when tortisses d'git 'ot they do spit poison like a snaake. Twould be the death of 'ee."

"Do 'em sure 'nuff?" ax Noah, drawing back all scared. I've never reed that in the tortiss book."

"Books doan't tell 'ee everything," says the maid.

"But wot can ther' do?" Noah went on, wriggling every way on the bed like he was setting 'pon a fuzzy-bush. "You've done a job of it you 'ave. Ee'll never be the saame no more. Twill maake me very bad - you must a-knawed wot would 'appen if 'e was took up agaain this cowld weather."

Mary was stooped down, watching the tortoise going along. "Ee seem to be trottin' round right as ninepence," she says.

"Tha's oal you knaw. Ee'll drop down dead any mennit, that's wot ee'll do. Ee's shaakin' on 'is legs, I can zee it. Pool lil thing! You o't to be hoss-whipped. Carr'n out now - go on!"

Mary did'n take no notice. She made a step towards Noah like if she was screwing up her courage about somethin'.

"That tortiss edd'n goin' back garden again till" - and she spoke deliberate, clinching her hands - "till you 'gree to laive me an Dick go courtin'."

Noah sit bolt upright like a poker. "'Ere! Thes edd'nt fair - usin' me poor tortiss fer yer awn ends! Merderin' me tortiss! Twas Dick Rawe put that in yer nuddick - gashly varmint! But 'ee need'n think......"

Mary glanced down to the tortoise, what had stopped short on the canvas, and she bite her lips. "Tortiss is stopped now like if ee caan'r go no furder," she gasp.

Noah glaazed and jerked down his head twice. "I towld 'ee so. Ee's dead."

"No, ee edd'n dead, granfer," says the maid putting out her hands towards un. "Frightened I speck. Tis up to you any'ow, an' I doan't think ther's no time to be lost. If you want to saave yer tortiss you mus' zay Dick can come in 'ere when ther's misletoe up, an' then go on wi'out the misletoe. You knaw wot I main."

Noah lied back in bed panting. "Aw right, aw right," he mumbled. "Fer saake o' me tortiss."

"But you mus' laive Dick come in 'ere fer company fer me every evenin' so long as you'm up bed. Do 'ee agree?"

Noah groaned. "If twill saave me tortiss - anything, anything!" he says. "But if ee should die I taake it oal back an' Dick Rawe sh'll never darken these doors. I doan't give in fer 'is saake, ner yours. You'm too bad, to play sich trick 'pon me. Now, maake haaste out and bury un up agaain nice an warm - ee may revive in onder the grounds. An' mind to put the board up over un. 'Ave 'ee left the 'ole open?"

"Iedd'n a very big 'ole, granfer," says the maid, walking round and round the tortiss and squinnin' at'n all nervous. "I'm nearly 'fraid to tich'n granfer - if ee should spet 'pon me...... Put yer 'ead in onder the bedcloas - ee might turn gashly if ee seed you."

"Never mind that. Tis yer awn fault. Carr'n out!"

"Put yer 'ead onder the bedcloas, else I woan't."

"Aw drat et!" snapped Noah, and ducked his head onder the sheets. When he looked up the room was empty, and Mary's footprints could be heard goin' down the stairs, then the outside door shut and Noah heard her staavin' out around the end o' the house. He lied still for a minute, then striggled up uneasy.

"Mus zee she do bury un up vitty," he says to himself. "I bet ee'll be dead afore she git up there - tis frewzin cowld. I bean't sure ee wad'n dead afore she carr'd un out o' 'ere, an' that's why she made me cover me 'ead up so I could'n zee un. Well, if ee is I'll knaw et, an' she an' Dick will be furder apart than ever."

Noah got out o' bed and pulled on his stockings, gasping terrible and sweat pouring over un. Very stiff he tread across the room to landing and then in back bedroom. Going fore to the winda he heed in behind the curtains and geeked out. His eyes bulged like saucers next minute.

Mary was standing in back garden path, waving her hand out over the hedge. Coming down the road from downses was Dick Rowe. There wad'n no sign o' no tortiss nowhere. The board was up where ee belonged, and it seemed to Noah that the earth had'n bin moved. He wrinkled his face into some shape and jerked his head too and fro some bothered.

"Blest if I can zee droo et!" he mumbled. "There's zummin on between they two. There she go - blawin' kisses to un! I'll look furder into et - they bean't goin' fool me!"

Forgitting his aches and pains he hobbled back to the landing, catching up his nightshirt, and tread over stairs. 'Fore he got half-way down he stopped short and his eyes glued theirselfs 'pon kitchen table. There - good lor! - she'd left the poor tortiss in on the table, leaning weak

Mained to murder un she did, from the fust!" cried Noah, grounjing his teeth with rage, "An' if ee's dead I'll go out to that Dick Rawe......"

In one jump Noah reached the bottom o' the stairs. With a lil screech he stanked fore and grabbed to his tortiss - then stand back like a man shet to.

Twas somethin' what Dick had bought in town two days afore - a toy tin tortoise, run be clockwork!

AN EXCITING WASH-DAY

'Twas early one Monday morning 'long in December that Mrs. Budge went in Pengooth churchtown for a packet o' bluin', what she'd run short of. She'd went in by main road, but having met Mrs. Skinner in shop she'd felt 'twas best to come back along the downses, so that she could let off some more steam. Flat road 'twas, with a old sand burra piled along one side, and over t'other end of the downs was a crossroads wi' Mrs. Skinner's house set 'pon the corner.

First-long there was some talk 'bout Mrs. Budge's bluin' and the bother o' extra washing for Christmas, but it could be seen that Mrs. Budge had somethin' else in her mind more important. And when they got half-way across the downs she out with it, stopping short in the road and rubbing her fat cheeks wi' the bluin' packet.

"Polly edd'n in no mood fer helpin' me at the moment," she says all mysterious.

"Aw," says Mrs. Skinner. "Took slight, is she?"

"Lil bit o' bad feeling, Mrs. Skinner. I'm hopin' twoan't last long. I want to git her fixed up wi' the right young man - git her away from that jinny-quick, Daave Goudge - never be nothin' 'e woan't, as I've towld her over an' over; but maids is so pig-'eaded! Teddy Perks is the one for her - smart eddicated chap, carr'in' everything in front of un like a steam roller. Lift our family a bit higher up if we can git Teddy in un." And Mrs. Budge flinked her head superior.

"H'm!" says Mrs. Skinner, very cool. "I tho't Teddy was gone away from Pengooth."

"So 'e is - went up be the mornin' train. Up Plymouth tis - got a fine job there it seem, an he'll be maakin his fortune."

Mrs. Skinner gave a lil grunt as they moved on, very slow, near treading 'pon one another's toes.

"Tis a risky job tryin' to git a maid in'trested in a chap wot edd'n there," says Mrs. Skinner. "A chap wot's to be see, Mrs. Budge, alw'ys git the preference."

"They could write love-letters," snaps Mrs. Budge, glaazen up at Mrs. Skinner, who was a good six inches the tallest. "An' she could go up an' zee un anytime - Plymouth edd'n far away. I knaw Teddy got a eye 'pon her - he've towld me so much in private conversation, an' if aunly Polly'd finish wi' thik Daave things would be settled fitty." Mrs. Budge stared for a minute around the sky, what was frosty and clear, then went on some vicious:

"Spiteful natured chap Daave is an' soonder er laater 'e'll be comin' out in 'is trew colours. He knaw I doan't faavour un and 'e's waitin' his chance to git 'is awn back. Mark my words." She gived a lil coughing noise afore laying hold to Mrs. Skinner's arm. Nobody in churchtown knaw wot I'm planning. You mus'n braithe a word, will ee?"

"Nit till I've seed fer meself," says Mrs. Skinner.

The two of 'em was now goin' down a nip towards the corner and both of 'em fixed their eyes 'pon the road a lil way below Mrs. Skinner's house. Lorries had been along there Saturday and upset a nub or two o' clay, and somebody'd bin and scribbled up the road wi' gurt old capital letters.

"Cheldern bin busy agaain," says Mrs. Skinner, sniffing. "They do purtly dirt up the roads when ther's clay goin' to an' fraw."

"Ave ee bin down an' read it?" ax Mrs. Budge.

"No; ha'nt bin that way over the week-end. Teddn nort, I don't speck."

Mrs. Budge looked s'picious and beginned stalkin' down towards the white marks. The letters had bin wrote from t'other side and she to walk over 'em and turn round afore she could read what was wrote. And she had a shock. They gurt old sprawly letters went like this:

"TO MRS. BUDGE - LOOK OUT - I'LL DEAL WI' YOU NEXT, FAT AS YOU BE."

Mrs. Budge blinked back to Mrs. Skinner and beckoned her wi' a stiff move of her hand. Mrs. Skinner come buckling down, and a minute later she was trying to kip herself from laffing out loud as she read the notice.

"That edd'n no child's 'andwritin'," says Mrs. Budge, awful quiet. Her hands were clinched and her double chin ded'n look quite so double - drawed in tight, like-a-thing, as if she was chucking. "I bean't decaved - I knaw it - tis saame 'andwritin' wot used to be outside envylopes when Polly got love-letters from Daave Goudge.

Mrs. Skinner frowned doubtful. "'E never wrot' the 'dress in capital letters, did a?" she ax.

"Nevr mind" - and Mrs. Budge waved the bluin' high over her

head. "I say I can see a resemblance - the way 'e do put in 'is dots - anybody could recognize - ess, tha's Daave's doin's so sure as daylight." And then, so sudden that Mrs. Skinner was fair frightened, Mrs. Budge beginned to rave.

"I towld ee so! 'E think 'e've got reds o' Teddy an' now 'e's threatenin' me. Right out 'ere in public!" She glaazed around desperate. "Wot can there do? Putt zand over it! Cover it up!" And she started runnin' towards the sand-burra like a maazed thing.

Mrs. Skinner screeched out, waving her arms: "Come back, Mrs. Budge - no good tryin' that. You bean't 'lowed to put sand on the roads. An' leave go o' that fuzzy bush - ee woan't 'elp - aunly get prickles oal ovver the rooad an' puncture people's tyres. I'd best go in fer me broom."

"Go on then!" yelled Mrs. Budge flouncing around wi' her face like a brandy bottle. "An' maake haste! Et mus' be brished up afore anybody zee et. Maakin' me a laffin-stock like that - I'd go flop where I stand if anybody reed sich things about me." She watched Mrs. Skinner limp away in and then stand on the writing, her lips bite, geekin' right and left, 'fraid she'd hear footprints approaching.

'Twas jist as Mrs. Skinner come fooching across wi' the broom that Mrs. Budge happened to fix her eyes 'pon a field gate further down the hill what she had'n looked to partic'lar till now. And her eyes went like bools.

"I declare!" she gasp, "If there edd'n more writin' - You clane up this while I go down and zee wot's marked on that gaate." She went off in some tare and was soon frecked in the gateway spellin' out the words scribbled right across the top bar o' the gate.

"TEDDY'S GONE PLYMOUTH, MRS. BUDGE, AND 'TIS TIME YOU WENT WEST."

On the next bar twas wrote:

"ME AND POLLY WON'T STOP AT NOTHIN' - LEAVE HER ALONE, YOU OLD NOSEY OR THERE'LL BE BLOODSHED."

For a croom Mrs. Budge could'n believe her eyes, then she give a shiver and catched hold to her head, lopping weak back agin the stone-gate-post. Mrs. Skinner tho't she'd gone faint and left her broom to some flying along and see what was up. She found Mrs. Budge lurrin' around so black as thunder and mumblin' away under her voice.

"'E need'n think 'e's goin' bate me be sich insulks," says Mrs. Budge. "I'll go over an' zee oal the fam'ly of 'em this very evenin', and 'av it out with 'em." She gave a kick at her neighbour who was looking a bit scared. "Giss on in fer scrubbin'-brush so as I can clane this gaate; an' if ther's any more of et around anywhere......"

But there wad'n. Mrs. Budge got home safe without any further upsets 'bout quarter hour arter.

Polly was setting 'pon kitchen table when her mother came in. Purty maid she was, wi' blue eyes and hair yella as butter. Mrs. Budge ded'n leave her 'ave a breathin' space, but boxed right fore and poked to her wi' the bluin' packet.

"You got to finish wi' Daave Goudge at once," she declared, panting away fit to burst. "Things 'ave come to a head this marnin'. If 'e railly loved ee he would'n insulk yer poor mawther as he 'ave."

"Why!" Polly gasped stiffening back 'pon the table. "We abben falled out. Wot've ee heard?"

"I've SEEN", cried Mrs. Budge, spreading her arms out and nodding her head up and down like an old rooster. "You'll find out soon 'nuff. I'm goin' over Goudge's to-night an' lave 'em knaw wot I think of 'em. You woan't 'ave Daave hangin' round ee no more, my laady. An now I mus' git on wi' me washin'."

This was a hint to Polly, but the maid ded'n take it. She glaazed to her mother all sulky and dabbed her hand to her eyes while Mrs. Budge was stooping down to lift the flasket o' cloas. Be time the woman 'ad straightened Polly was making tracks for the passage leading to the parlour.

"Bean't ee goin' help me wash?" Mrs. Budge shout arter her.

"No," says Polly. "You'm alw'ys - alw'ys tryin' to do zummin." And creedling in front room she slammed the door.

Mrs. Budge was in a temper all the morning and scat goin' the washing in fine style. Twad'n bad weather and she reckoned she'd be able to dry the cloas afore evening. She'd got it hanged 'pon the line braave an' early, mumbling threats as she drived the pegs in, scowling across to the Goudge's house, what stand 'bout fifty yards off, t'other side of a 'lotment.

Polly stopped in front room and ded'n even leave it fer denner - would'n ait nothing, she said, if Mrs. Budge ded'n changer her mind 'bout goin' over Goudge's in the evening.

Tay-time come, and jist arterwards, when Mrs. Budge was wiping up the dishes, she happened to geek out o' kitchen winda. She glaazed for a spur, then give a jump what told that she see'd zummin special, and poked her head in round the curtain. A minute later Polly heard her start gabbing to herself, some old rigmarole.

"I'm beggared! There's Daave Goudge come fore 'lotment to burn up that ole stroyl. Ess, 'e's raakin' of it an'..... wot's a doin' now? I caan't zee fitty fer they gooseberries. Taakin' matches from his pockit, b'lieve - ess, drat the fella! No, 'e's aunly lightin' his pipe - I tho't 'e would'n daare...... Ess 'e is - stoopin' ovver that stroyl! Wot!" Mrs. Budge banged open the winda and holla'd across in some flurrick:

"I've 'ad 'nuff imperence from you oalready, Daave Goudge. I bean't goin' waaste words. You laive that go till 'morra. Caan't 'ee zee I got cloas 'pon me line?

Daave straightened up and glaazed back at her. Strappin' gurt chap he was, and he ded'n look much bothered.

"Ess, I can zee et, missus," he says, very quiet. "But wind edd'n blawin' that way - no smoak would'n titch yer cloas. I'd a waited, but tis lookin' a bit rainy an' if the stroyl got wet again we could'n burn it for days. I want to git et out o' the way - gurt ole whack o' weeds like that - anybody might tumble over it and kill theirself if they was comin' long 'ere in the dark."

"Who's goin traapse 'cross yer 'lotment in the dark?" axed Mrs. Budge, scoffing.

Daave waved his pitchfork and turned his back to her, taking zummin more out of his pocket. Mrs. Budge squinned home her eyes and beginned grumpin' away again to herself.

"Now wot's that 'e's pullin' out of his pockit? Paper o' some sort, edd'n it? Ess - Polly!" She raised her voice, tossing the words back over her shoulder. "E's burnin' o' yer love-letters - envylopes an' oal! There they go on top the stroyl - wan, two, dree, fower - eight of 'em!"

"Caan't be," come Polly's voice from paalour, all choky. "I never send un more'n six."

Then tus somebody else's too, an' you'm well rid of un. I bet e' bin flirtin' shameful - got love-letters from haalf the maidens o' Pengooth." She bawled out again to Dave:

"Doan't you dare put a match to that there 'eap! Insulkin' me in public rooads is bad 'nuff, but if you smutch me clain cloas there'll be another 'count to settle when I go over your plaace d'reckly. I give ee the warnin' I bean't freckened o' yer threats."

Dave wriggled around the stroyl with his pitchfork; it seemed to Mrs. Budge that he was grizzling.

"I'm sorry if ted'n convenient," he says, very 'umble, "but I'm 'fraid it caan't be 'elped now. Yer cloas is near dry be look of it - could'n ee pick it in now?"

"O't to be out fer another hour itt, an' I bean't goin pick it down to plaze you ner nobody else. You think you'm the boss o' the shaw, but I'll shaw ee. Light that bunvire an' I go straight over an' inside your doors. Ther'll be ructions any'ow, but tis wuth et to git Polly saafe out o' yer hands. Do ee hear that?"

Whether Daave heard it or no, his next move could'n be mistook. Very cool and deliberate he stooped again, strik' a match and light the bits o' paper in onder the stroyl.

Mrs. Budge lift her hands in horror.

"There! 'E've done it!" She slammed home the winda and went raging towards front room. "Oal right - better 'ave it over! If Mrs. Goudge come to blows wi' me she'll find I'm the best man."

Jist as she got to passage the paalour door opened and Polly come out. She was pale, her eyes were flashing, and she grabbed hold tight to her mother's arm.

"Go over an maake a split between me an' Daave," she said gulpy, "an' you'll be zorry for it so long as you live."

"Doan't ee be so fullish, chiel. The split's come oal-ready. Giss on up to Plymouth an' you'll be right on wi' a better chap than Daave Goudge could ever be."

"Teddy Perks!" says the maid sneering. "Pooh! I would'n look at that ole baaby-faace!"

"Well, I'm goin' over Goudges' like it er lump it. Tis fer yer awn good. You can zee foer yerself 'ow spiteful Daave is - out there smeechin' up our clain cloas, yours so well as mine - an' if you'd aunly seed the insulks 'e wrote......"

Mrs. Budge flounced back to the stairway, making for the bedroom to put on her hat and coat. The stair carpet had been took up to give things a sort o' spring-cleaning for Christmas, and the boards was bare. One of 'em, 'bout half way up, was a bit rotten and lately they'd always minded to step over un when they was goin' up and down. but Mrs. Budge was in sich a flurry that she ded'n think 'bout that rotten board. Stamping down her feet wi' all her weight 'pon un ee gived away, an' next thing Mrs. Budge knawed her legs 'ad gone right down droo in the spence. A gurt stug o' pig's fat stand zackly in onder, and she went plunk right in it while her hands laid hold to the banisters. Soon's she'd steadied herself a bit she yelled like mad:

"Polly!"

The maid come running in from passage and had a fitty shock to see her mother's face white in behind the banisters, what she was clawing away to like a old cat.

"Good lor, mawther!" gasp Polly. "Wotever be doin'? Wot've ee done?"

"Thikky stair bin an' broke," screech Mrs. Budge, streggling to pull herself up droo the hole. "Come up an' 'elp me, caan't ee? I caan't git up. I caan't move me legs. Polly! I'm sinkin' I'm in the pig's fat. Haale me up, caan't ee?"

Polly went up a couple o' stairs, then stopped and shaked her head.

"Laive yerself go, mawther, tha's best way. You caan't git back to stairs agaain - you'm gone too far. Try to git yer feet on zummin solid - only mind yer head as you duck in droo the hole."

Mrs. Budge left go o' the banisters and very slow she went out o' sight, splinterin' the wood right and left as she slithered and wriggled herself down. No soonder was she gone than she made some screech.

"Polly! Open the spence door! Tis dark as a sack down 'ere, an' I b'lieve the bottom o' the stug is come out - ee caan't be so deep as this. Tis up to me knees - Polly! Quick! I be stagged up to me knees in lard an' caan't move hand ner foot!"

As Polly made to open the door Mrs. Budge flinged out her arms to try and grab hold o' something, but instead she scat over a bowl o' water on a shilf. When the door opened Polly seed some sight of it - her mother streaming leakin' wi' the water she'd untipped, striggling to git her feet up out o' the lard, waving her arms around and scatting brooms and saucepans right and left along the wall. Polly made to step in, but Mrs. Budge waved her away.

"Taake up that water fust - 'ave the floor-cloth! Look at et - goin' right 'cross kitchen - an' tha's new carpets there!"

When Polly came in wi' the pail Mrs. Budge was still flouncing around in the stug, looking more and more frightened.

"I doan't b'lieve I can git out," she gasp. "Tis so thick and jammed oal round me legs so tight - an' cowld this weather, like a chunk o' ice frewzin to me bones." She turned 'pon Polly some vicious.

"Oal your fault! 'Ow ded'n ee mind me 'bout thikky stair? You knawed ee was rotten. Turned ghastly you be, like Daave Goudge, an' doan't desarve the good I'm tryin' to do ee......"

Afore Mrs. Budge could git any furder there come a knack 'pon back door, and heavy footprints was heard. Next minute Dave hisself was stanning in kitchen doorway, looking purty anxious.

"Who's murdered 'ere? he axed.

The maid stepped towards un, smiling shaky. "Nobody - 'ad a accident er two," she says, pointing in the spence. "Stair gived away - lucky you was outside."

Mrs. Budge craaned her neck to git a geek at Dave, and nearly made the stug topple over. They heard her splutter zummin what sounded like: "You clear out o' my 'ouse!"

"No, 'e mus' stop 'ere, mawther," says the maid, grizzling to see how the tables was turned, "to lift ee out. You caan't loose yerself else -tis sticked around ee like glue, an' my arms bean't strong 'nuff to lift sich a ton weight."

Dave put his arms round Polly and gived her a squeeze, then a bright idea came to un and he ducked fore so that Mrs. Budge could see un.

"I'll haive ee out," he says, "the mennit you promise to laive me an' Polly go courtin' fitty, wi'out any more o' these upsets."

"I never will!" yelled Mrs. Budge, rocking to and fraw in the lard.

"Then you'll stay there oal night," ansers Dave, cool as a cucumber. "I abben done ee no 'arm, you knaw I abben, an' there's no sense......"

"Who wrot' they insulks on rooad and gaateway if twad'n you?"

demanded Mrs. Budge. "Prove that you never done that an' you can lift me out - but you never will proove it. I aunly got to look at yer faace to knaw who threatened me wi' bloodshed this marnin'. You bin out blackenin' me cloas now, an' you'd black me eyes if you 'ad 'aaf a chance. Teddy Perks......"

"Jist a tick, mawther," says Polly, holding up her finger and stepping to one side. "There's somebody else listenin'."

Very quiet the front door had opened. Mrs. Skinner was stanning in the passage.

"Zorry to shuv meself in," she says to the maid, "but I tho't I'd slip over an' laive yer mawther knaw a bit o' news what's badly needed, be the looks of it. My maid Barbara was out pon the sand-burra yesterday, and she's sayin' now tay-time that she seed Teddy Perks writin' on the road, 'bout fower o'clock when ther' wod'n nobody about. Towld me of it 'erself - I had'n axed, ner said nothin' 'bout no writin'. So there you be! Ted Perks could'n be trested - clever foakes never can...... Ane anything 'appened 'ere?"

Dave coughed and then took a step towards Mrs. Budge. "Shall I lift ee out?" he axed, very polite. "Will ee laive Polly an' me alone?" Mrs. Budge groaned, but she nodded.

CHARLIE, THE SMUTTIES AN' THE BAABY

"Look heere, Charlie," sed Bill Tremlett to his sen wan tay-time; "we'm renned out o' virin', an' the cooal-an-stick man woan't be heere till beginnin' o' nex' week."

"Aw," ses Charlie; "wot do ee want me to do - stale some?"

Owld Tremlett stamped hes veet in onder the taable. "Course not!" snaps he.

"Dunnaw where we can borrow any," ses Charlie, hes mouth vull o' saffern caake.

"Borry? Wot do ee think I'm mainin' of? I doan't want ee to borry nort."

"Aw," ses Charlie; "wot do ee want me to do, then? You reck'ns we aan't got no virin' in to go on tha week - tho't you mus' main fer me to git some somewhere."

"So I do, you thickhe'd! Smutties. Plenty out 'pon downs. I want ee to go out'night an' git a barra-load."

"Be meself?" ax Charlie. "Ow caan't you go?"

"Caase I'm busy," snaps hes faather. "Now, look sharp an' 'ave yer tay, then go right out an' git a pile afore et come in dum."

Charlie pulled foare his cup an' empt out the tay en hes saucer. He ded'n veel in no mood fer spendin' a hour en tha freezin' cowld out 'pon downs, and jist nibbled away to his caake, glaazin out tha winda, hopin' as 'ow twud come en dark foare he finished tha mail. The owld man seed wot Charlie was on 'pon, and oal of a sudden, as Charlie howld the saucer up to hes mouth an started zoopin away, he gived un a scat en tha elbaw. Up went the saucer an' tha tay skit out oal ovver Charlie's faace an' down hes waaistcooat drenchin' of um fair laikin'. Charlie glaazed ovver the empty saucer, mouth oppen; gone red as a beet he was.

"Wat tha diggens do ee think you'm doin' of?" he spluttered, knackin' me like that!"

"Maake haasts an' finish yer tay," answer hes faather, taakin' up a noospaper from the binch beside un.

Charlie seed twas no good to try an wriggle out o't, so he jist shuv'd back hes plaate an' rised up. His cooat was streamin' an' he went foare to the vire to dry un, sticken' up en frent the stove, glowin' sideways 'cross at tha owld man en be'ind the paaper. Bill ded'n sed nawthen - jist went on aitin'.

D'reckly Charlie maade to go out an' zet to work. "Wot mus' I bring 'em hom' en, faather?" he ax.

"I towld ee, ded'n I? - A barra-looad. You'll vind un out en tha linney."

Charlie nodded an' retched fer hes cap 'pon a nail in the kitchen beams. Arter he'd put un on he steck'd glaazen at owld Tremlett a mennit or two, bestin' whe'er to go or no, arter oal. Bill glanced up from hes noospaaper an' waaved a arm.

"Urry up, do ee heear? I want they smutties in afore dark; they mus' be in cooal-house be time mawther come back from town six o'clock, else there'll be ructions. Tha barra - "

"Dang the barra!" ses Charlie. An' ee mained et.

He creedled out with a idaya in hes mind; he was grizzlen wicket as you-mind-to.

The linney was a li'l freck of a plaace out beside tha houze - li'l owld shanty weth a roof vull o' hoales an' a brok winda. Charlie went 'cross to un an 'flinged oppen tha door. Enside twas gittin' dum a'ready an' he cud hardly zee proper wot was there. He catched sight o' the barra handles sticked up ovver a lime-bucket, an' stanked foare to grab 'em. Twas some job of et to git the thing out, fer the floor was in some pickle, ess fi! There was wood boxes an' jam-pots an' pails - oal strewed aroun' any'ow, and the wheel o' tha barra was catched in be'ind a saucepan weth a cabbage in un, an two turmuts. Charlie haaled to they handles some foace, and oal of a sudden the contraption gived away. Ovver went a box vull o' earth, right on top of a jam-pot, scatten of'n ta sherds; ovver went tha saucepan an' cabbage an' turmuts come rollin' 'cross the linney, bunk agin Charlie's veet. He'd bin pullin' so haard he cud'n saave hisself, an' back he went too, wallop on the floor, weth tha barra on top of un. Fer a mennit he tho't twas oal up wid'n and then he veeled a earthy cabbage-stump up gin his noase an' was 'fraid hes faather wud be comin' to see wot 'ad 'appened. En two ticks he was on hes veet an' fumblin' aroun' on the binch inside tha door tryin' to find wot he wanted. He vound it. Li'l while laater he was trundlin' the barra out past tha gaate-way ento the rooad. Ther was a hammer heed inside hes jackit.

Zackly as he got to rooadway the door oppened an' out come hes faather.

"Wot was oal tha kick-up jist now?" ax he.

"Nawthen much, faather. Barra got catched, tha's oal."

Owld Tremlett waaved hes arms. "Mind owld fella," ses he, "else you'll git catched. See?"

Charlie ded'n anser. He squitched hes hed t'other way and stalked off weth tha wheel-barra en frent of un. He knawed that hes faather mained wot he sed an' was in two minds fer a mennit 'bout tha idaya wot 'ad come to un. But twas cowld goin' long tha rooad an' a braave wind was risin'. Charlie shivered 'tween tha handles, thinkin' o' bein' sticked up fer haalf-hour pon the oppen downs. "No!" ses he to hisself. "I'm goin' risk et!"

Soon's he got out o' sight o' tha houze - loanely spot twas where he lived - he dropped tha barra en tha middle o' the rooad an' turned aroun'. Nobody wad'n lookin'. Charlie grizzled to hisself. He wud see ef tha owld man wud boss un like thes or no! Stoopin' down he grabbed the handles agaain and scoot foare to a gaate-way. Behind un come the barra, bouncin' like a rubber ball an makin' 'nuff row fer a steam-roller. Once he'd got en the lew o' tha gaate-way, he cluckied down en tha cordner an' pulled tha frent o' tha contraption aroun' to meet un. Then he grabbed the wheel an' haaled to un. That ded'n do much, so Charlie dipped in hes inside pockit an' drawed out tha hammer. An' then he zet to work.

Vew mennits laater he heeard footsteps comin' long the rooad - a man's walk be the sounds of it. He went quiet as a mouse, howldin' hes breath. Twas too laate - tha man 'ad heeard tha hammer goin' 'an hes he'd come pokin' aroun' tha cornder o' tha hadge.

"Hullo! You is et, Charlie? Barra broak down?"

Charlie glaazed up ovver the wheel, purtly flustered. He knawed tha fella - Marky Grigg, Susie Grigg's faather. Charlie knawed Susie Grigg - had fer months. They was courtin'.

"Ess," ansers he. "Summat gone wrong weth tha wheel heere - twoan't taake more'n a mennit, though - "

"Anything I can do ta help ee, Charlie?"

"Ther' edd'n," ses Charlie, oal quaavery. "Thanks oal the saame, Maaster Grigg. How's Susie?"

"Aw, right's ninepence. Gone ovver to see Tommy Biddick's missus tonight - goin' put tha baaby out far a ride en that pram, I reck'n." Charlie spet. "Any'ow I'll see her 'morra. Tes oal right 'bout that wheel-barra, Maaster Grigg - I'll 'ave un den in vew ticks. Good ebenin'!"

When Marky had passed 'long, Charlie got up an' geeked 'round the hadge corner, maaken sure that owld Grigg 'ad gone out o' sight afore he zet to work agaain on the barra. Ded'n taake but a jiffy then fore tha treck was done.

Ten mennits laater Charlie come up to the gaate outside hes plaace, draggin' a barra weth a wheel inside of un. Tha hammer he'd flinged ovver the garden hadge be'ind - he'd put ee in tha linney d'reckly. Hes faather 'ad heeard the thing scroungin' long tha rooad, an' wondered wotever twas comin' - no sound o' wheels, aunly like a piece o' timber draggin' along. He come out en some flurrick.

"Wot do this heere main?" shouts he, rennin' down to gaate. "Wot've bin den ta my wheel-barra?"

"Wheel's come off faather," sed Charlie, oal waik; he lookied some whisht there weth tha thing trailin' be'ind un. "Dunnaw 'ow et 'append - I was trooklin' behind 'un 'lon tha rooad an' oal of a sudden tha wheel wobbled away in front an' I tumbled fore wallop caase tha theng wud'n go no furder. See 'ow I cut me faace - ee's bleedin'." That was trew nuff - but Charlie 'ad dun'd et out en tha linney when he went sproalin' mongst the jam-pots.

"Be you tellin' tha trewth?" ax owld Tremlett, flingin' oppen the gaate an' stankin' out to where Charlie stand.

Charlie jerked his he'd down. "Wheel bin loose fer aages - you knaw ee 'ave, faather. I've towld ee heaps o' times - "

"Doan't mind et, thun," snaps tha owld man.

"Tha's yer mem'ry, faather - you knaw tes failin'. I've towld ee scores o' times you caan't mind things like - "

"That'll do!" Bill kicked to a stoane en tha rooad. "Wot 'bout me smutties?"

"I was thinkin' tha saame, faather," ses Charlie, laivin go the barra. "Caan't go now ee's broak up. P'raps 'morra - "

"No 'morra 'bout et, me sen! You laazy lout - tryin' ta wriggle out o't, be ee? You doan't best me, owld fella! Go up downs fer smutties - go on!" Tha owld man pointed; he was shaaken oal ovver like a jelly.

"But faather, how can I? I aan't got nort to bring 'em hom' en."

"Got yer arms, aan't ee? Git a gurt yafful, that'll last us on till end tha week. An' git a move on, too - comin' en dark soon. Never min' 'bout this contraption, I'll carr' et in."

Poar owld Charlie creedled away like a dog tail-piped. Twas no good fer un to try any moare trecks. He 'ad ta vetch tha smutties and tha soonder he got tha job ovver tha better. He heeard hes faather haalen tha barra up the path an' round' ta the linney. Then he runned like vire up towards tha downs nearly quarter mile away.

Jist as he got there he catched sight o' somebody comin' 'long the rooad en frent. Somebody pushin' a pram and cheel squalin'. Charlie's knees wobbled, fer he seed who twas. Susie Grigg! Good job he had'n started pickin'.

"Well, Susie," ses he when they drawed level; "Out weth Jaanie Biddick's baaby again?"

"Ess," answers the maid - purty she was, smilin' up to un - grey eyes and nice browny haair onder a blue an' yella tammy-shanter.

"I seed yer faather jist now," ses Charlie, glaazen aroun'. "He sed you was out weth tha cheel. Purtly squallin', edd'n a?"

"Ess, I dunnaw wot to do by un. He want hes dummy. An I left un be'ind. Tes whisht goin' long like thes heere."

"Awful," ses Charlie, waggen hes he'd down at the mite en tha pram. En some tantrums tha cheel was, yowlen 'pon top of hes voice. Could heear un couple mile off, he was maaken sich a bal. "Ought ta do summat, Susie. Why people will think you be tearen tha beggar up ef he go on like thes."

"I knaw," ansers she, oal des'prit. "But won can I do? He woan't stop till he git hes dummy, an - " She broke off; a tho't 'ad come to her. "Charlie, will you - do ee mind stayin' heere weth un while I ren back fer tha owld dummy? I woan't be long - I'll go like the wind, an - "

Charlie was in some fix fer a mennit; he tho't o' the smutties an wot hes faather wud say if he ded'n git 'em. But weth the cheel maaken sich a hollabaloo he ded'n 'ave much choice 'bout wot he wud do. "I'll wait, Susie," ses he, "aunly doan't kip me heere fer long - I'm 'fraid me life the pleece'll come long, thinkin' I'm tryin' to chuck un or summat.

Susie laffed. "Doan't you worry, Charlie - jist stay heere an howld tha pram. You can wheel un aroun' to kip out the cowld. Doan't ee scoald un - he'll aunly git wuss." And 'way she went back ovver the downs.

Charlie had never bin en sich stank as this afore. To be parked up there en the cowld weth somebody else's baaby yowlen nuff to splet hes ears and not knaw wot to do to passify tha cheel' - aw, twas tarrible for un, an' when Susie'd gone out o' sight he veeled like turnin' tail and bowlten off out of et.

Vive mennits passed long and then ten - still poar Charlie was frocked up, and the baaby squallin' wuss than evver, if any odds. He veeled maaze nuff to scat to un, an' thinkin' o' they smutties maade et wuss for un, cause twas darkenin' in braave raate and ef he ded'n start pickin' soon -

Twas like a flash that the tho't come to un. Ther' was a way out! He wud mind the baaby an' pick hes smutties to tha saame time. The pram was a owld wan, weared out - a wisht poor contraption. If he wheeled un en cloase 'gin where the smutties was to - . Suitin' action to tho't, Charlie got be'ind the pram an' beginned to shuv. Now a pram edd'n zackly like a wheel-barra fer pushin', an' Charlie vound tha thing rennin' away from un amoast till he got to tha bumpy part in on the downs. He amoast jousted tha poor baaby's life out an' the li'l mite was grabbin' howld to the sides and yowlen out som'n awful. Any'ow, Charlie did manage at last to git the pram in cloase agin tha burned fuzzies an' steppin' li'l bit to wan side he beginned to break 'em off. En a croom he 'ad so much as he could howld en hes han', and stanked back to the pram an' laid 'em sideways

69

'cross the bottom. Then he went for 'nother lot an' done the saame thing by they. Some plaised weth hisself he was. "So good's a wheel-barra," tho't he, an' went on looaden up till he'd got a proper whack o' virin' on top the pram. Tha cheel was still screechin', and howldin' hisself back like in onder the hood - 'fraid o' the smutty sticks a s'poase.

Charlie glaazed to un, wonderin how much longer Susie was goin' be; then he maade to wheel the looad back to rooadway. Twas then that he seed wot a job he' done for hisself. He had'n got a yard afore the wheels bunked up agin a stoane, and the sticks fall'd fore, right in on top tha baaby. The cheel's faace an' eyes was plastered weth smut, an' his li'l woolly 'at was spotted up shockin', an' so was hes baid-cloas. Charlie was some flustered; he steck'd there, sweaten' like a sheep an' shaaken like a jelly.

"I've done et now," ses he to hisself, and he glaazed aroun', tryin' to heed hisself in be'ind tha pram. He ded'n daare go no furder, tha cheel wud be smothered in smut; as twas he was coughin' of et up as ef twas chuckin' of'n.

'Nother ten mennits an' he catched sight o' Susie comin' - good way off, right ovver other end of the downs. But be that time he was worked up to such a pitch he cud'n stay to faace her. Laivin' pram an' baaby an' smutties he scoot back to tha rooad an' down tha hill to hes hom'. Hes han's an' cloas was smutted up an' ther' was straiks od it on hes chacks where he'd dabbed at the sweat wot was trooklin' ovver 'em.

When he got to gaate he vound hes faather steck'd outside tha linney. Twas purty dum, but he cud maake out the shape of un and see that he was howldin' summat. His 'eart amoast stopped as tha owld man come stewerin' out, flurrikin' the hammer!

"Come back agaain be ee - an' wethout tha smutties! I'll taich ee, you lurgy young iggit! I knaw wot you dun'd. Jist vound this wan up en garden path. Ee wad'n there tay-time. You smashed tha barra an' tho't I shud'n vind out ded'n ee? Well you'm bait...... An' where's tha smutties, owld fella? You got smut oal round ee - you bin pickin' of 'em? Where be em to, hey?"

From up the downs ther' come the sound of a cheel screechin'. Charlie grooaned, but he cud'n anser.

HUMOROUS VERSE

LIGHTER VANE

I've never been called a weathercock;
    Folk pictured me as a grim old rock;
But that's absurd, for I always spun
    When a frisky wind said, "Time for fun."

Above the pews, above the bells,
    The rooster dances as it tells
Which way the climate's veering round
    To scorch or drench the lower ground.

And now, it seems, the ageing vane
    Twirls brighter in the sun or rain:
Someone has reached it - bless the saint
    Who gave it a new coat of paint.

THE CATCH

When Ruth, my wife, was a child,
And London said in its strident way:
"Hurrah! Today is Bank Holiday,"
She would trek, if the weather smiled,
To the Epping fringe, a little river,
With her Mum and brother and sister.
Ignoring the reek and blare of the fair,
The shouting herd in sports fields and parks,
She pursued her private larks.

She dangled a jam-jar on a string,
And thought of tiddlers wriggling,
Minnows darting, ripples parting
As the round glass struck and sank.
She could imagine sardines and trout,
Or even a dolphin leaping about -
Too big to catch in a jam-pot,
But good to look at when you're feeling hot.

Oddly enough, it was there
Amid the seclusion and fish,
With her loose dark hair
Holding stems and pollen from trees,
That she got her first squeeze
For a newspaper splash.

A reporter and camera-man,
Hunting Bank Holiday titbits,
Came suddenly on the scene,
And scooped for their local paper
The dignity of her bare
Scratched limbs and hauled jam-jar.

"Little girl, you've caught a whopper,"
One of them said to her.
Prophetically,
He must have meant *me*.

PUSHING THE BOAT

When Auntie Bella pushed the boat
    She made the squirrels hop,
And on our table, day by day,
    The ice-cream landed plop.
While Bella pushed the boat out
    The treats would never stop.

O squirrels made of chocolate!
    O ice-cream made of frost!
We ate them, warm or chilly,
    At Auntie Bella's cost:
Because she pushed the boat out
    We'd pulled out from dry crust.

SHELL DISPUTE

A mermaid rang up Cerris
    On the 'phone from Lundy,
Saying she had missed some shells -
    Must have them back by Monday.

"I did not pinch them," Cerris said;
    "I am an honest fairy.
If they are yours I'll post them back,
    But I distrust your story.

"You say these shells are treasures
    Given to you by your granny
In a cave beneath the sea,
    But that sounds too uncanny.

"You say you left them on the beach
    To trap some filching tourist.
You say your husband spied on me,
    And that he is a florist.

"I bought some orchids in a shop,
    And giant dandelions:
My pockets bulged with shells - they showed
    As innocent as buttons.

"The man was nice - no spy, I'm sure;
    Besides, his wife was present.
You're not his spouse - you have no feet.
    Why are you so unpleasant?"

SISTERS

Naomi was a chimney-sweep
    In a fancy dress affair;
Sharon was an angel,
    So they made a perfect pair.

We need more sweeps and angels
    To clear away our soot -
To poke the brush or bring the hush
    That makes us clean and cute.

A LINE ON MY NIECES

Yes, "Mandy" rhymes with "candy,"
    But she's outgrown that approach.
No, her hair isn't sandy;
    No, she doesn't live at Roche.

Yes, she is going steady,
    And keen on her hairdressing course:
No, he isn't called Teddy;
    No, her Mum's not a nurse.

Yes, she has got a sister
    As fair and fresh as a rose;
But that sounds trite - let's be crisper
    And say she enjoys disco's.

Yes, they all call her Maggie;
    Yes, she is fond of verse;
She did once throw grass tufts at me,
    But nothing worse.

Yes, they're both clever and quiet;
    No, they would never touch drugs:
They are sensible in their diet,
    And don't go down with the mugs.

SNOW LINGO

Peter built a snowman
    And tried to teach it French,
While his sisters watched and listened
    On a frozen bench.

The lesson made small progress,
    The snowman seemed obtuse:
Its green hat never nodded,
    Its mouth stayed mute and loose.

A parrot or computer
    Would show a keen response,
But a snowman is too harmless
    To have a lot of sense.

"Mon frère," said Peter kindly,
    "My brother...." Then a whizz!
The snowman's arm was pointing:
    "Your sisters - there they is!"

The children were quite startled
    To hear the snowman speak;
But it never grasped translations,
    And it melted in a week.

CONNECTIONS

This house, to which my love-letters were sent,
Switching on the safe current
Of comforting emotions,
Has now been equipped with North Sea gas,
So I am scared of explosions.

At my desk, a few yards from this North Sea
Gas, I write letters courageously,
Transmitting no fearful sparks;
And my friends, reading my lines amid safe fuel,
Feel cosy and sing like larks.

BADGERS IN WEYMOUTH

So my adopted home
Is now beset by badgers. That's a problem:
How can I cope with them?

My eyesight's not too good:
I could not chase a badger through a wood:
I wouldn't shoot or club it if I could.

I'm hazy in my badger lore.
What do these animals devour?
What is in danger when they're lurking near?

In Castle Gardens, say,
Would they eat roses, gnaw the palm roots, try
To beat up goldfish or a butterfly?

Perhaps they just make bumps like moles,
Or spoil the lawns with irritating holes.
This, too, alarms me: there's the risk of falls.

Are they maliciously disposed
To poets and the elderly? I've closed
Our doors. I'm quite brave, but confused.

CHOUGH STUFF

"What's a chough really like?" asked Sharon.
    "A pity I never saw one.
It isn't a Dorset bird,
    And it's getting scarce, I've heard;
But it's here on my badge from Cornwall,
    Looking sweetly warm and small.

"The cloth makes it soft and fluffy -
    I'm sure this bird isn't stuffy
Like an old owl; but it's black.
    Does it sing or scream or quack?
(I want to know what sort of noise
    Is made by other things than boys.)

"I shrink from black things as a rule -
    They're often dismal, daft or cruel.
But this badge.... oh, I can take heart
    From Auntie Bella's blackberry tart,
Ask her to take me down to Newquay
    And feed the choughs - if they're not too rooky."

TANK TOUR

Jonathan told me he climbed a tank
    As part of his holiday tour:
At five a gun can seem good fun
    Until you hear it roar.

So Jonathan climbed the sleeping tank
    And eyed its joints with glee,
The shining metal where flies would settle -
    Perhaps a scornful bee.

His sister meant to be a nurse;
    She watched him, her pride turned queer:
If he lost his grip, if his foot should slip,
    He would need her skill - oh, dear!

She stepped up close and raised her hand
    To guide him around a muzzle,
But he screamed out: "G'wan! I'm a soldier man.
    Go home to your jigsaw puzzle."

LANE TRAFFIC

Not many cars in our ramshackle, ungroomed lanes
When as a clear-eyed boy I stole,
Sometimes ran, to the road and stared
At a farmer on horseback, or slow-moving wheeled things -
A sprightly jingle bouncing on its springs,
Bright shafts fencing the nimble pony;
A harvest wain, sweet-smelling with its tower of hay,
Or a gipsy caravan, moored for a few minutes
While an exotic dark woman with bangles and baskets
Wheedled in a cottage doorway.

There were also industrial monsters:
The belching brute-bulk of a steam-roller
Making the ground shake; the daily shuttle
And shuffle of clay-waggons, piled with white cubes,
An iron drag fixed against one wheel
To ease the team going downhill;
More rarely, an incoming load of empty casks,
A fantastic yellow pyramid, strapped on a dray,
The tiers of bulging wood dwarfing the horses
Which sweated on their last lap to the kiln.

RETIRED

Now I'm a Senior Citizen,
    But I've a junior wife,
And so I don't feel crabbed with clay
Or its wrinkled strife.

I draw enormous pensions,
    Though my home is mini and wee;
And soon I'll sail from Exeter
    With a hon. degree.

I wear some heavy pullovers
    As my retirement starts,
But on my wife's warm birthday
    I'll sing for shorts.

Into my clay-cut harbour
    Glide blithely, at rare times,
Three birds whose whispering fingers
    Add zest to my rhymes.

I don't need booze or snooker
    To keep my wits in trim -
Only a romp, a walk in the rain,
    A book and a hymn.

There were knots in the gaunt old hamlet,
    But my line grew straight and clear:
I guess it will keep me perky
    For a greener sphere.

LANDROVER

It looks almost as elegant
As a grandfather elephant,
And gives you more of a shock
Than a rumbling grandfather clock;
But it's the ideal means of transport
Over civilized ground of that sort -
Rutted lanes and strewn stones and
A lot of bumpy industrial sand.

You have to lift your leg high to climb in,
While the vehicle vibrates like sin.
Once inside, you wonder whether
The seat is made of gravel or leather:
It won't hold you up, it slants to the floor,
Getting your bottom cramped and sore
As you slip and hoist and slip again,
And grab at the driver's seat in vain.

You're pitched to and fro against metal points,
Your head hits the roof, bars jog your joints:
You see the landscape spin and bob
With the lurch of the wheels as they do their job,
Gripping the grit and spluttering round,
As fierce as a tank: their bullying sound
Is somehow part of the fun. I tried
To feel a kid's gusto in that ride.

BOOTS

So here, on his way to the screen,
      Is a poet in Wellington boots:
Such a marvel has rarely been seen,
      For it doesn't fit fairies or flutes.

I cannot imagine poor Poe,
      Or Arnold or Keats or Clare,
Kicking their way through this slough
      In the big floppy boots I now wear.

The mud is alarmingly thick,
      And my wife clings tight to my arm
As the movie cameras click
      To catch the incredible charm.

We wade on our rubber-shod feet
      To an excavator, now stuck,
All crusted with sand, dripping wet,
      Near the rim of the ripped claywork.

On request I scoop mud in my hands:
      My wife tries to keep a straight face:
Our comedy always expands,
      Even in this bootiful place.

CHRISTENED AGAIN

Zoe brought a doll called Anna
    To my christening service;
I was ripe as a banana -
    Over sixty - and sort of nervous.

My wife sat in the pew,
    Anna perched on my knee;
We were out of the TV view
    With Zoe, off duty.

The folk being filmed, dressed up
    Quaint and antique, like,
Watched my start, kept their zest up,
    Sang at the sleek mike.

I had a space-man feeling
    As a real live baby
Took my name without squealing.
    Was the clock back? Maybe.

I felt young enough for kicks,
    All gurgly and sprinkled:
That's how a poet ticks,
    Even when he's wrinkled.

IT'S ONLY ACTING

We're grouped in a lane
In a smudge of rain
That fits the scene we are shooting.
Young Liz plays the part
Of my first sweetheart,
Who nearly gave me a booting.

Oh, how many times
She has mocked at my rhymes
In staging the perfect rehearsal!
And soon on telly
I'll shake like jelly,
My suit in rags of dispersal.

She brushes me off
Because I'm no toff -
I've nothing but verses to woo with.
Her nose in the air
Makes me smell the despair
Of a guy she'll have nothing to do with.

To think of old flames
Who called you names
Can prompt a whimsical pleasure.
What I aid and abet
While I'm getting wet
Is watched by my wife, my treasure.

FILM RIGHTS

Young Cerris ties me up with string
    Till I am handcuffed to my chair,
But soon relents and lets me feel
    The soft long freedom of her hair.

Zoe has outgrown such strings and things;
    We just have tickles before tea.
"I saw you in a magazine,"
    Her finger whispers happily.

They played together in my film,
    And now, off-stage, they can relax,
Disclosing in my haunted room
    Their unrehearsed endearing knacks.

With string and tickles, love and fame,
    I am the richest guy extant:
My shabby youth was pickled - yes,
    But here's a jolly extra slant.

FEASTS

Zoe jumped out of the butcher's van
        Because she saw a mouse:
It nibbled at the pork and beef
        Before she reached my house.

She called for Kate and Gina too,
        And also Uncle Stone,
But when they came the mouse had gone
        And only left a bone.

How different was the London feast
        Which Uncle cooked with care!
In that nice flat without a rat
        We all enjoyed our share.

And then we watched the lovely film
        About some girls and boys,
And Cornish pits and poet's fits
        And cars that made a noise.

And after that we caught a train
        And rode a long, long way:
With chips and pranks we all gave thanks
        For such a splendid day.

Then back at Goonamarris
        Strange happenings followed fast:
I was no mere clown in a dressing-gown,
        But a real robed star at last.

No mouse or butcher climbed the tip,
        But a huge card sailed to land -
From Zoe and Kate, to congratulate,
        While Gina chirped on my hand.

IT JUST SHOWS

When I bounced back from London
        With lipstick on my cheek,
My wife she wasn't jealous,
        She didn't think me weak,
For we were in the art world
        Where all the folks are warm -
The good *religious* art world
        Where hugs can do no harm.

We featured in a film there:
        It had a lofty theme -
A love as softly melting
        As Cornwall's best ice-cream.
Our base that day was Weymouth,
        And there my cheek was scrubbed:
My wife was laughing - oh, so proud
        That hubby wasn't snubbed.

VIDEO

Down by the dark stair-post,
As sudden as a ghost
A small hand touched me, comforting like toast.

Young Sharon said, "Hello!
You've got the video:
We need it at my uncle's for a show.

I'll lead you to the car -
It isn't very far:
I'm proud of you now you're a real film star."

I hugged her and said, "Why,
You're certainly not shy.
You'll keep me safe: I think the weather's dry."

Outside, the Weymouth street
Was cosy - sea air sweet:
No cats or badgers tripped my guided feet.

I clutched the precious spool
Which held my nightmare school,
My bandaged face, the girls who acted cruel.

I'd left all that behind,
Though others saw it: blind,
I screened a caption: "Darzet maids be kind."

WESTWARD - WOW!

Naomi looked westward from Saltash bridge,
Her foot tapping Cornish dust;
She flicked away a Devonshire midge,
Wrinkled her nose in a pixie pose,
And said: "Oh, Mum, we must -
We *must* go all the way
To the fairyland of clay!
I must see those funny stacks,
And have tea at Uncle Jack's."

"The fairy mounds all over the place
Will fatten and change shape
While I eat my jam and pinch his face
And pull him around the queer white ground,
Pretending an escape.
We'll scramble up a hill
(How high does the sugar spill?
I mean the sand). It's sweet
To give him such a treat."

Naomi looked up at the gravel peak
That sparkled above Bloomdale.
The hot car stopped and the magic streak
Spread wide for Jack on a brambled track
As she made it a fairy trail.
They didn't need any jam,
Or even picnic ham -
Just felt at the Cornish end
That Dorset sweets could extend.

BOARD SCHOOL

To Reggie the village school was hell,
    The blackboard a brimstone blank,
So he stole away to the railway siding
    Under a claywork bank.

He was filled with awe and wonder,
    Passing the line of trucks,
Each with its bright painted message -
Education *de luxe*.

There were coal trucks in from Cardiff,
    Clay trucks from Staffordshire:
He could picture the grim Welsh headstocks
    And the delicate china ware.

"Here's my geography lesson:
    You always learn better outdoors,
Without a teacher." Reggie was right -
    Before television, of course.

FLORAL CLOCK

Kate stared at the postcard I'd sent her:
    A bright floral clock was shown.
I'd explained that its hands were dripping
    Through a shortage of towels in town.
"Could you spare a rough towel, dear Katie?
    The hands stay so dreadfully wet,
They don't set a good example
    To kiddies, or even a pet."

Kate shook her dark head. "I'm sorry,
    I can't let him have one - I daren't.
You can't trust a man with a towel -
    He rubs till the skin's half burnt.
I'm struck by this clock in the gardens -
    I agree it's been over-washed,
But how could he dry its face and hands
    Without every flower getting squashed?"

A WAY OF TICKING

I knew a poor village couple
　　Who would never observe Summer Time:
To make the hands of a clock tell lies,
　　They said, was a wicked crime.

So the old grandfather was wound and oiled,
　　But its hands were left alone:
It rumbled and chimed the solid truth
　　In December as in June.

The wooden clock on the mantelshelf
　　Stayed loyal to G.M.T.,
And the round metal clock in the bedroom
　　Was taught no trickery.

That couple could get away with it -
　　No kids, no radio;
They never used a bus or train,
　　Or ventured out to a show.

Of pubs and sports and churches
　　They took a wintry view;
And, stuck inland, they needn't ask
What time high tide was due.

NYMPH-IN-WAITING

That student's from abroad - she's in distress:
Wildly she scans the beach,
Distractedly she flinks her hands.
She wants to dress,
But her kit has vanished from the sands.

She rushes to and fro, grabs people's arms,
Implores in broken speech:
"Where aire my theengs... my slacks... my cloos?
It come of harms...
Stole... melted! Find police! I lose."

Folk try to soothe her, or they think she's queer;
They all survey the strand -
The aunts and grannies guarding toys,
Bags, towels. It's quite clear
They're innocent. The thieves were boys,

Or spiteful girls, or pals - just for a lark.
Let's hope they'll soon relent.
She cannot board a bus or tramp
The streets so stark:
Cold drops leak from her - she'll get cramp.

NURSERY

The coal-shed sparked off paradise
    When Saturdays were wet:
    We felt marooned, and yet
The thumping downpour made us laugh,
The grimy cell looked snug and nice -
    So far from the school staff.

We were like chimney urchins there,
    Little Lorraine and I:
    We felt so warm and dry
Except when, sailing on the swing,
Our legs shot into open air
    And caught the splashing sting.

We had our swings in turn: the best
    Was when I stood behind
    And saw her form outlined
Against the clouds, beyond the door,
Curving back to be pushed and pressed
    As she bumped my hands once more.

Sometimes we climbed the pile of logs
    Or slithered on the coal,
    Or made a bottle roll
Through cobwebs thick as apple tart:
Her hair, thick as a golliwog's,
    Lit up my infant heart.

STREET CAROL

As soon as Naomi began to sing
    Under the lamp-post, the light went out.
She gasped, but close by in the dark
    Her brother Paul gave a cheery shout:
"Five minutes more there'll be a moon,
    So carry on with your tune."

"Good King George walked down this street
    On the feast of Chesil,
When the cats crept near the fire
    To watch the chestnuts sizzle,
And barrels stood outside each door,
    Full of...." Here Paul cried: "Encore!"

"You interrupted," she complained;
    "I forget what the next word is.
Oh, is it 'gunpowder' or 'bran,'
    Or is it simply 'fizz'?
Please let me sing. Don't go away."
    Paul grinned and said, "Okay."

But suddenly they saw the moon,
    And everything was altered.
Naomi said: "Let's go home soon:
    Those barrels never mattered.
I want mince pies, not that old king.
    Besides, there's no-one listening."

DIGGINGS

"Only the old inhabitants can help,"
Said pioneering Kate.
"Our school gang wants to excavate
The village rubbish dumps
You can't see now because of bramble clumps.
We'll clear the sites and dig for bottles
Long buried under docks and nettles.
These antique bottles make us yelp,
The way archaeologists do
When they find relics of a zoo
Or Roman tiles in Timbuctoo.
I know, it may seem bunk,
But are there bottles where you tipped your junk?"

I answered: "Sorry, Kate,
The bottles aren't quite clear
In my memory, I fear.
I often carried a pail or bath
Up a little roadside path,
And emptied the soot, torn paper and rags,
Tins with tight lids or cruel jags
Which had let out food for my plate -
Corned beef or treacle or sardines,
Oxo, pineapples or beans.
I also threw down peelings, greens.
But I can't mind a single bottle -
Perhaps 'cos I was reared teetotal."

SLAG VISION

Frosty dusk at Bloomdale, where a high-perched engine-house
Had snorted and spat cinders over the tip-face.
The woman and boy, wearing threadbare raincoats,
Bent cheerfully at the black base.

She dropped her zinc bath among bushes
While he rattled an empty pail,
Starting to climb through the shale.
Her voice, deep and Cornish, warned him:
"Only put in the cherks, not the clinkers:
Clinkers went burn." He made no reply.

He plied his sifter, scooping and lifting
The crisp flaky slag, tossing aside
The stony or iron-red bits
That wouldn't burn. At times he whistled,
Feeding his pail, shifting his foothold,
Sinking till his boots were swallowed.

But when he turned to take the load down,
His shoulder sagging and aching,
He noticed his mother, grew aware
That she was patient among pyramids,
That the pyramids strangely framed the pit-head,
That something about loneliness and nightfall
Was spilling, kindling as it spread
On the raw crust of his poet soul.

BIRTHDAY TREAT

When bright little Ruth, there at Chiswell,
    Gave big Ruth a monkey,
Carved, tiny and hard as a nutshell,
    We beamed in our glee.

Young sister Rebekah came running
    To sing "Happy Birthday":
They sang to my wife till Aunt Bella
    Cried: "Bed-time! Away!"

The two Ruths had guided me safely
    Up wooden steps bouncing,
While summer light danced on the garden
    And the sea's nimble fling.

No monkey tricks ruffled that evening
    Of blithe celebration:
Ruth's monkey slept on in the handbag
    As we climbed in the sun.

EPILOGUE: CHORUS OF THE CHILDREN

You've heard of the Cornish curmudgeon,
    That surly, cantankerous chap
Who scowled at the flowers in dudgeon,
    Or growled at a kid on his lap.

"How awful to meet Mr. Clemo!
    He can't hear a word that you say:
His speech is restricted to 'Hem!', 'Oh!'
    And 'Yah!' as he drives you away."

We beg to inform all and sundry
    That this is not true of him now:
His manner has ceased to be thundery,
    He has learnt to say 'Honey' and 'Wow!'

And even in his fame's epidemic
    You'll find him astoundingly calm
As you hinder his ode or his epic
    By writing small talk on his palm.

GLOSSARY OF CORNISH DIALECT

A

allis	always
ascrode	astride
ax	ask

B

bal	bawl, a loud noise
balling	hammering, (The 'a' is pronounced as in 'bat').
barra	wheelbarrow
bestin'	defeating, getting the better of
bluin'	blue chemical for rinsing clothes
bobsididow	a violent quarrel
bool	ball, a fat person
bowlten	bolting
braave	fit or good
braithy	breathe
brindle	to become angry or annoyed
buckle droo	bustle through, walk or act briskly
bunk	bump
burras	burrows - i.e. clay-dumps

C

chacks	cheeks
chiel or cheel	child
chow	chew
chuck	to toss or throw
cloas	clothes
cluckied	stooped or crouched
cluffing	squatting
clunk	to swallow
clunkers	muscles used in swallowing
core	a shift or working schedule for labourers
crame	cream
creedled	crept
croom	a short space of time
cuddy	a rough hut or shelter for workmen
cut abroad	opened or severed

D

daggin'	longing, desiring
deery	dairy
den	done
doodled	wrapped up, heavily dressed
downses	downs, open common or waste land
drekly	presently, later on
droaks	ditches or gutters
droo	through
duffan	dunce or idiot
durn	door jamb or lintel
duffed	flipped or smacked

F

ferm	a bench
fitty	proper, fit, suitable
flasket	a wicker basket
flounce	to shake or jerk the body
flurrik	fluster
foare	forward
fooched	slouched
foxin'	pretending, deceiving
freck	to stand; also a pitiful-looking person
frizz	splutter in anger
fuzzies	charred furze twigs
fuzzy-bush	furze, gorse bush

G

gaakin'	staring
gabbin'	gossiping
gashly	ghastly, spiteful
geek	to glimpse or look closely
giss	get
glaazen	scowling, peering intently
glowed	frowned. (Pronounced to rhyme with 'proud')
gone poor	rotton or contaminated
gounjing	grinding
grizzled	chuckled
gummock	simpleton
gurt	great

H

haaled	pulled
heed'n	hide it

hettin'	warming, heating
holding abroad	opening wide
holla'd out	shouted
hurtin' of'n	hurting him

I

iggit	idiot
inyun-house	engine-house

J

jaaced	chased
jank	prank
jinny-quick	a stupid or careless person

K

kick-up	rumpus, disturbance
knack	knock

L

lampered	spotted or thickly covered with dirt or a rash
lew	sheltered
licker	misfortune
linny	linhay, a small shed
lopping up agin	leaning against
lurgy	lazy or tired
lurrin'	grimacing, scowling

M

mane	mean
mawther	mother
mazed	mad, furious
minse	mine
missment	mistake
mit	met
mizz-maze	confusion, bewilderment
murfles	freckles
mykies	mica tanks on clayworks

N

nex'	next
niffid	annoyed
ninny	a fool
no cop	no good, useless
nort	nothing

nuddik	head
nuff	enough

P

penny-liggen	penniless
pindy	mouldy or decayed
plat	small open space or patch of ground
pleece	police
plosh	a bog or marsh
pluffy	soft, over-ripe
plunk	headlong
pooching	pouting
purty	pretty
pussed out	pursed out, spent
putcher	pitcher, earthenware jar for water

R

renned	ran
rowl	roll

S

saffern	saffron
scat	to hit or knock
sclow	scratch
sen	son
shada	shadow
sherds	pieces, fragments of broken crockery, etc.
shet to	shot
sifter	a small shovel
sim	seem
skiddering	sliding
skit	skip
skittery	slippery
slocking	enticing
sloojed	slouched
smeech	unpleasant odour or grime
smutch	to smear or soil with smoke, etc.
smutties	clumps of twigs blackened by heath fires
spence	cupboard under stairs
spet	spat
splain	explain
splat	splashed
sproalin'	sprawling
spur	space of time
squabbed	sat or squatted

squallin'	whimpering or crying
squeezed home	shut tightly
squilch	squelch
squinned	squinted, peered narrowly
squitched	twitched or turned
staaved	hurried, walked fast
stagged	covered with mud, heavily overworked
staling	stealing
stanked	stamped or strode
stet	stoat
stewerin'	flustered, in haste
stiddy	steady
stroyl	dead garden weed raked into heaps
strub	to rob or destroy
stug	large earthenware tub or jar

T

taare	rage
taaren	rushing
tail-piped	shorn of its tail
taisy	irritable, bad-tempered
tay	tea
tearen	tearing
teddy-oggy	potato pasty
thews	those
thikky	that
titched	touched
toall	at all
toatlish	senile
traade	material
trammin'	taking loads in clay-trolleys
trookled	trickled
turmut	turnip

U

ussel	throat

V

vinnid	mouldy, decayed
vire	fire
virin'	fuel

W

wicket	wicked or roguish
wisht or whisht	in poor condition

witnick	a witch or mad person
wuss'n	worse than

Y

yafful	armful, a bundle filling the grasp
yowlen	howling

Z

zoop	to suck